CLOSE ENCOUNTER

Gunn was still groggy from a deep sleep when he opened the door to find the luscious Jilly smiling up at him.

"Jilly, are you sure you know what you're doing?"

"I know. I got cheated once—I don't want to be cheated again."

She stood on tiptoes, kissing him and making a purring sound in her throat. Her tongue slithered into his mouth, sending a shock of electricity through him. He kissed her hards, overcome with a sudden desire of his own.

"You don't want this, Jilly. I'm no gentleman."

"I want you, Gunn—that's all that matters."

As her hands urgently stroked and caressed him, a hot fire shot through his loins. He kissed her brutally but she didn't retreat. His hands ripped off her gown to expose her soft, young flesh.

While he carried her to the bed, he asked again, "Why?"

"I have to find out something. I'll tell you later."

"That may be too late. You can't go back, you know. You won't be the same."

But Jilly was too enraptured with his lovemaking to hear what he said . . .

MORE EXCITING WESTERNS FROM ZEBRA!

THE GUNN SERIES BY JORY SHERMAN

GUNN #12: THE WIDOW-MAKER   (987, $2.25)
Gunn offers to help the lovely ladies of Luna Creek when
the ruthless Widow-maker gang kills off their husbands.
It's hard work, but the rewards are mounting!

GUNN #13: ARIZONA HARDCASE   (1039, $2.25)
When a crafty outlaw threatens the lives of some lovely
females, Gunn's temper gets mean and hot—and he's got
no choice but to shoot it off!

GUNN #14: THE BUFF RUNNERS   (1093, $2.25)
Gunn runs into two hell-raising sisters caught in the middle
of a buffalo hunter's feud. He hires out his sharpshooting
skills—and doubles their fun!

THE BOLT SERIES BY CORT MARTIN

BOLT #6: TOMBSTONE HONEYPOT   (1009, $2.25)
In Tombstone, Bolt meets up with luscious Honey
Carberry who tricks him into her beehive. But Bolt has a
stinger of his own!

BOLT #7: RAWHIDE WOMAN   (1057, $2.25)
Rawhide Kate's on the lookout for the man who killed her
family. And when Bolt snatches the opportunity to come to
Kate's rescue, she learns how to handle a tricky gun!

BOLT #8: HARD IN THE SADDLE   (1095, $2.25)
When masked men clean him of his cash, Bolt's left in a
tight spot with a luscious lady. He pursues the gang—and
enjoys a long, hard ride on the way!

*Available wherever paperbacks are sold, or order direct from the
Publisher. Send cover price plus 50¢ per copy for mailing and
handling to Zebra Books, 475 Park Avenue South, New York,
N.Y. 10016. DO NOT SEND CASH.*

GUNN #4
BLOOD JUSTICE

JORY SHERMAN

ZEBRA BOOKS

KENSINGTON PUBLISHING CORP.

ZEBRA BOOKS

are published by

KENSINGTON PUBLISHING CORP.
475 Park Avenue South
New York, N.Y. 10016

THIRD PRINTING

Printed in the United States of America

DEDICATION

For Leslie,
who has both
vision and
patience.

CHAPTER ONE

Gunn rocked in the saddle, dozing. Half-asleep, he followed the trail along the American Fork, in Flathead country. They were calling it the Clark Fork now, but the old-timers still called it by the old name. He'd been riding since daybreak, trying to make Dixon before nightfall. Get in some kind of bed.

He heard the sounds just as he emerged from Hell Gate Canyon.

Then, the world exploded in his face, jarring him awake.

A lone covered wagon rumbled straight at him, smoke and flame belching from the rear.

On its heels, a screaming pack of near-naked Indians rattled rifle fire at the wagon. Blackfoot.

Gunn wondered what in hell Blackfoot were doing in Flathead country.

He wondered for only a split second as bullets

began frying the air in his direction. Balls of hammering lead whistled and spanged all around him. Gunn kicked his horse in the flanks, scrambled for cover. A lead slug sizzled past his ear and he felt his spine crawl with a nameless fear. He jerked his Winchester .44-.40 from its scabbard as his horse scooted off the trail, haunches low, its hind hooves digging in, rooting the earth of rocks and sand in twin sprays.

The wagon skidded and careened sickeningly as one of the two horses pulling it was shot out of its traces by a warrior riding close to strike coup. The other horse shied and screamed, its eyes wide enough to show the whites. The wagon's wood whined in protest as it came to a rumbling halt, vulnerable to the Indian attack.

Gunn began picking targets out of the pack, shooting from the saddle. He zeroed in on a Blackfoot rushing to kill the other horse. He squeezed off a shot. The Blackfoot threw up his arms, flinging his rifle high in the air. The Indian hawked a cry of surprise and fell out of the saddle as if jerked by an invisible string. The Indian's pony crashed into the remaining horse, causing it to bolt and begin pulling the wagon in an aimless circle. Again, the horse went wild-eyed as it saw its dead companion, now a brown hulk acting as a fulcrum on which the wagon turned. The wagon tongue ground into the dirt, plowing a furrow, further frightening the horse. The shooters inside paused, as if reloading. Then, the rifles began to bark again from vantage points between the canvas and side panels.

The man called Gunn tracked another Indian racing toward the back of the wagon. He gave him two feet of lead, squeezed off. The Blackfoot's face exploded in a cloud of blood. He tumbled backward out of the saddle, landed in a sitting position, stone dead. Gunn took out another, racing from the opposite side. Low. The shot took the pony in the haunches, twisting it around so that the horse's forelegs jerked up short. The Indian flew over the withers, sought the ground in a gravity drop, embraced it sadly with outstretched arms. What was left of the wind in his chest pushed out of his throat in a *whump* of expulsion.

"Aieeeeeeeeeeah!" screamed a Blackfoot who had realized, suddenly, that there was another enemy shooting at them from the rocks. Rifle fire from the wagon tore the Indian's chest open, splaying ribs and breastbone to bloody splinters. The Indians, seeing that they were taking fire from two directions, began to mill and retreat. Gunn made sure they got the message. He leveed shells into the chamber, firing as fast as he could pull the trigger. The wagon, too, laid down a withering fire. There were five Indians left. Demoralized, they choked off their war cries and began retrieving their dead. Gunn stopped firing. The wagon, too, held fire as the Blackfeet picked up their lifeless brothers.

Their mourning wails hung in the air as they retreated up the river they called the Big Blackfoot. The last rider stopped momentarily, turned to hawk his indignation at the wagon. Someone inside fired a shot that fell short, but spurred the red man to follow his companions.

A stillness hung in the air.

Gunn patted his horse's neck, calmed him down. "Ho, buck," he said. The buckskin snorted. He was wedged into the rocks. "Come on boy. Easy, boy." Buck moved. Gunn ticked spurs against his flanks. The horse kicked free of the rocks, pranced back onto the trail warily.

Gunn rode up to the wagon, curious.

"Hello in the wagon," he called. "You all right?"

The ugly snout of a big Sharps poked through the canvas. Gunn's scalp prickled.

"Drop your rifle. Get off your horse."

"What?"

"You heard me. If you don't want to be blowed out of that saddle, you'll do what I said."

The Sharps jutted out an inch or two more as if for emphasis. Gunn heard an ominous cocking noise.

He let his rifle slip through his hands, dropped it to the ground as gently as he could.

The voice.

It was old, creaking. Male or female, he couldn't tell. Odd accent. He climbed off his horse, stood there feeling helpless, exposed. The .50 caliber muzzle glared at him unwaveringly. Whoever was behind that barrel was a fair shot. And, at this range, he had about as much chance of outrunning a bullet as a buffalo had of growing wings.

"Drop yore gunbelt, too. Hurry up!"

He unbuckled his belt, let the holster touch ground before dropping the belt. He felt naked, vulnerable.

"Get his stiff, Jilly. Step lively."

A young girl, or woman, dressed in striped black trousers and a man's linsey-woolsey shirt, leaped out of the wagon as sprightly as a nymph. The Sharps stayed aimed at Gunn's throat. Steady as a rock. The girl, her black hair flowing past her slim waist, picked up Gunn's rifle and gunbelt. She held a pistol in her hand, an ugly Starr double-action .44 Army. She looked as if she knew how to use it. She kept the business end aimed at Gunn's gut as she backed up to the wagon and threw his rifle and pistol inside.

The canvas flap jerked up suddenly and Gunn saw the owner of the Sharps.

An old woman, dressed in a granny outfit, complete with bonnet and bustle, climbed out. Gunn saw that the wagon was no more than a converted buckboard. Light, fast, small, but sturdy.

"Keep them hands up high," ordered the granny woman.

Gunn figured her to be at least sixty years of age. Maybe less, maybe more. Her wrinkled skin was delicate as parchment, but her blue eyes crackled with icy fire. The young girl possessed those same sparkling eyes. The old lady was spry, agile. She bounded down off the wagon, prodded him with the heavy octagonal barrel of the Sharps. It was too much gun for such a slight woman, but she handled it as if it weighed no more than a broom, carrying it light as a feather in thin, sinewy arms. She had a face like those he remembered back in Arkansas on Osage Creek, before the War, when he was a young man helping his pa on the family farm.

The old woman spat. The gob of snuff juice

spatted next to Gunn's boots.

"Get on outen the way," the granny said, pushing the rifle barrel into his gut. She stood off from him appraising the tall, gray-eyed man. Her flashing eyes swept over his broad shoulders, his leanly muscular body. He stood six one in his stocking feet. His dark brown hair was slightly shaggy, just above shoulder length. "Bit 'un, ain't ye?"

Gunn said nothing. His eyes were on the girl.

She stripped his horse of everything but the bridle. She didn't bother with neatness, but flung the saddle, blanket, bedroll and saddle bags helter-skelter over the ground. She tied Buck to the rear of the wagon, then went to the front where she began struggling to get the dead horse out of the rigging. When she had unbuckled the straps, she led the other horse out of the way, leaving the dead horse free of the traces.

The granny continued to eye Gunn as he watched the girl lead his own horse to the front and strap him to the harness. Buck didn't like it. She gentled him down then. He admired the way she had with horses, the expertness with which she had managed the change.

"I hope you know they hang horse thieves out here," he said quietly.

"You shet yore mouth," said the granny, shoving the Sharps at Gunn for emphasis.

Gunn's eyes narrowed. The old woman meant business. The Sharps was at full cock, her finger in the trigger guard. He had no wish to be blown apart by the .50 caliber ball shoved with anywhere from ninety to one hundred forty grains of powder. He could always buy another horse if it came to that.

"Jilly, you 'bout ready?" The old woman spoke to the girl in a different tone of voice than the one she had used with him.

"Hey, what about me?" Gunn asked. "I saved your lives! Those Blackfoot would have taken your scalps if I hadn't been around."

"Bullshit," said the old crone.

"Hell, lady, you can't just take my horse without asking."

"Get in the wagon, Jilly. We'll be on our way directly." The girl climbed in, sorted out her reins and waited for the granny.

"Come on, Grandma," she said. The first she had spoken, Gunn thought wryly. Her voice was musical, fluid with a soft southern accent.

The old woman scrambled up on to the seat. Jilly kept him covered with the Starr until her grandmother was seated. Then she put the pistol on the seat while the granny leveled the Sharps at him once again.

"Hey, you going to leave me out here? Take my horse? Hell, those Blackfoot could come back. I mean, after all . . ."

"After all," said the grandmother, "we need that there horse. Them Injuns done shot one of ours."

"How come those Indians were chasing you anyway?"

"Because, young man, we stole the two horses a-pullin' this wagon from them!" snapped the old woman.

Jilly cracked the reins. The horses wheeled.

Gunn coughed as a cloud of dust enveloped him,

clawed at his lungs, gritted his lips and teeth. He squinted up into a brass-bright sun, estimating the time of day. Maybe one o'clock. He was glad he had eaten. There was grub in his saddle bags, but not much. Dry biscuits, some jerky, a can of peaches, one of tomatoes. The wagon disappeared out of sight, but at least it was headed down Clark Fork toward Dixon. That was his destination. He'd be a little later getting in than he had planned.

He looked at his boots with chagrin. They were hardly fit for walking. The California saddle was too damned heavy to lug over rough country and that far. He'd have to leave it. He was unarmed, too. It was almost fifty miles to Dixon. He'd have to sneak through every inch of it if he wanted to keep his hair. Crow, Blackfoot, Flathead—hell, there might even be Sioux in this country! Those Blackfeet were miles from their home, raiding into supposedly "tame" territory. And, they were riled up if those women had really stolen two of their horses.

He examined his situation. He could buy another saddle and horse in Dixon. He had made enough in the gold fields to tide him over for a long time. Most of the money was banked, but he had notes, letters of credit and coin enough to sustain him. It was about a two day walk to Dixon, if he kept at it. Maybe he'd get lucky and a stage would come by, but that was unlikely. There was no regular stage route between Virginia City and Dixon that he knew of. Still, there was always the chance that someone in a wagon would come by on the way to Oregon.

The Blackfeet had retrieved their dead, but they

had not had time to pick up the fallen rifles. Now, Gunn walked over the brief battleground. Near a pool of drying blood, he found the old Henry .44. It was empty and he had no ammunition. He cursed, carried the rifle over to a large rock near the mouth of the canyon. He smashed the stock and banged the barrel until it bent. It made him sick to do such a thing, but it was better than giving the weapon back to the Blackfeet intact.

He walked over to where the other Indian had fallen. There, he had better luck. The Indian had been carrying a Winchester carbine. Made in '66, this one was more serviceable. It had a twenty-inch barrel, pitted and worn. The bluing was gone. He levered it quickly. Half a dozen shells fell onto the ground. He picked them back up, wiped them on his shirt. The shells were old. Bredan primers. They'd probably fire, though. He felt better. The action worked well. The rifle reeked of a foul-smelling grease. It would have to do.

Gunn walked back to where the girl had stripped his horse. He hefted his saddle bags and blanket onto his shoulders. At least they had left him a canteen. He slung that over his arm, after taking a healthy swig, and set out for Dixon.

His feet hurt, just thinking about the journey ahead.

His head hurt trying to figure out why two women would treat a man that way. A white man at that.

CHAPTER TWO

A man can walk four miles an hour if he keeps at it steady.

Gunn was trying to push six and he had been at it barefoot for the past half hour. A mistake. His feet were tender. He was a man accustomed to the saddle. On foot, he was like a fish out of water. He stopped, slipped socks on bloodied feet, crammed his sore feet back into his boots. He winced when he stood up. Cringed when he began to walk again. He was taking the hard ground, trying to keep his tracks to a minimum.

He envisioned a pail of hot water, salts to soak his feet in. A bed to lie in; a pillow to rest his head on. He had been on the road for five hours and he knew he hadn't come twenty miles. Close to it, maybe. The sun hammered him in the face even though he had his hat brim pushed down over it. It seemed to burn through the brim and scorch his face until it felt as raw as his feet. There was no breeze, no trickle of air in the August heat. The carbine weighed forty pounds, the saddle bags fifty. The bedroll drooped over his shoulders was like a wooden cross. The canteen strap ate at his shoulder like some gnawing beast.

He kept on, following the arc of the blazing sun. Hoping that the wagon would break down, that he'd find it somewhere ahead, the women weeping and wailing, gnashing their teeth. He'd love that! The women! The damned women!

Ever since his wife, Laurie, had been brutally raped and murdered two years before, Gunn, born William Gunnison in Fairview, Arkansas, in the year of our Lord, 1844, had found nothing but trouble with women. He wondered, sometimes, if he hadn't been born under a curse. Or, if Laurie's death hadn't twisted him in some strange way so that he always ran into troublesome women. As if his lower mind, the part that boiled up in dreams when he slept, didn't seek out such women to punish him for what he had let happen to Laurie. Yet he no longer blamed himself for his wife's death. Those who had been responsible had long since gone to join her. Coker, Caroline, the whole bunch of them.

Yet his path, since leaving Colorado Territory in '72, had crossed that of many women. South of the border, in the gold fields of Grasshopper Creek, Alder Gulch, Bannack, Virginia City. People wondered why he didn't settle down, had asked him why he was heading west when he was already a rich man. He knew why. The women. Wherever he settled for a time, the women found him. Some of those women were now dead, struck by the same odd fate that had blown out Laurie's flame. He knew it was nonsense to think that he was the cause—but the glaring truth was that many of the women he had known physically had come to violent ends. Through no fault of his own, but merely because they had been involved with him.

Now, these two. These two strange women. One an old granny, the other a young woman, a slip of a girl. He had not sought them out. They had come out of nowhere, chased by a pack of redskins, and he had tried to help them. To show their gratitude, they had stolen his horse, taken his weapons and left him afoot. To die, if not from knife or gun, then from sore feet. The bitches! He hoped to hell they'd break down along the road so he could cheerfully strangle the old woman within an inch of her life and paddywhack the young one until her bottom burned like cherry coals in a branding fire!

The trail edged away from the Blackfoot to join with the St. Regis and he knew that his thinking was worse than wishful. It was downright senseless. Those women were long gone, with at least one good horse to pull their goddamned wagon. The Indian horse hadn't looked puny, either. Dammit!

Gunn, once Captain Gunnison, who had fought in the War Between the States when he was hardly old enough to leave home, walked down to the St. Regis River which followed the Northern Pacific rail line, to fill his canteen. That act probably saved his life. He was soaking his feet in the cool waters when he heard them.

His hand went to his side, then he remembered his

18

pistol was gone. His hand rested against the handle of his Mexican knife, a gift from a man he had once befriended. Then, he realized he had only the carbine. The sound of horses grew louder. Gunn grabbed the carbine, crawled up on the bank, hid in the thicket between a pair of rocks.

The five Blackfeet had tracked him. Now, milling there on the trail where he had left it, they were speaking animatedly. One or two of them were using sign. He watched them, envying their mobility on horseback. He felt like a barefoot salamander caught out in the open away from the dark security of a hole. He had six shots in the rifle. Any or all of the old bullets might not even fire!

The leader of the Blackfoot seemed to be a young warrior with a single eagle feather in his braid. Painted and wearing only a loin cloth, the others listened to him as he gesticulated toward the river—toward Gunn's hiding place. As he watched in horror, they fanned out, came straight at him. Two of the men leaned over their barebacked ponies' withers and looked at the ground. It was easy. He had left tracks a blindman could follow.

Gunn waited, not ready to jack a shell into the chamber. Another mistake.

Keep coming, he said to himself. *I want one of those horses, you bastards!*

The leader stopped up short, slid from his horse. He made quick sign to the others. Gunn guessed at the range. Better than two hundred yards. Two-fifty, maybe. Close enough. If there had been a breeze he could have smelled them. They could have smelled him.

It didn't make any difference. They knew he was here.

The leader jerked his horse sideways, got behind him. The others dismounted quickly, did the same. They walked their horses expertly, keeping the animals between themselves and his position. He could see their legs every once in a while, but not their torsos or their heads. They had now fanned into a large u-shape, the leader farthest back. They could enclose him in a pincer movement once they reached the bank.

The Blackfoot braves moved slowly.

He knew they would have read the sign back at the mouth of the canyon. Read it like a book to a white man. They would know that the women took his horse, that he had smashed the Henry and taken the Winchester carbine. He wondered, though, if they knew how many bullets were in the rifle. They would probably know that there were some. So, they knew he was afoot and they had tracked him down. Five of them. And they were willing to take some risk to get him. Take his scalp home. They had none hanging from their belts. And two women had stolen two horses from them. They couldn't go back with that humiliation hanging over their heads. They had to strike *coup* on someone in order to save face.

On someone.

Him.

Still, they came, holding their horses' heads just right so that the animals had to sidle toward him, crablike. Their actions were a perfect demonstration of horsemanship. The plains Indians knew their horses, utilized them expertly. Gunn could not help

20

but feel admiration for them, even though he knew he was not likely to get out of this alive.

As they came closer, Gunn could see that they had not hurried after him. There was no telltale glistening of sweat on the horses' backs. He gathered that the braves were all young, probably renegades from the tribe, bent on proving themselves good warriors by reverting to the old customs. That made them doubly dangerous. These men were desperate. They would not go back to their home camp without a brave story to tell.

Two hundred yards and closing.

Gunn slid his rifle up into position, a scant inch at a time. His palm went sweaty. He dared not show the barrel until the last instant. Then, he would have to cock and take aim quickly. He would have to kill on the first shot. And the second. And the third . . .

As he watched them, Gunn began to build a strategy. Such as it was.

The Indians had repeating rifles. That much he knew. He could stand no chance against them in a rifle duel. They all stuck close to their horses' forelegs, using the neck, chest and legs for cover. He had no clear target of any Indian. The leader was the man he wanted most badly. Yet he was the farthest away.

The others listened to him. They obviously did what he told them. How would they act if he was no longer in the picture? Would they panic? Would they scatter? Come charging at him all at once? Which one should he try to take out first? The closest one?

There was another problem.

The ground was broken between him and the Indians. There were rocks and boulders, brush and flatland. It would only take one or two Indians to get him if he let any of them get away. He had six shots. Maybe.

There was only one way he stood any chance at all.

The strategy was formed.

Quickly, quietly, Gunn smeared dirt on the barrel of the carbine. The bluing had worn away to the metal. Once he shoved the barrel up, the sun would dance off it like a boxful of mirrors. The warriors would have him pinpointed and boxed. The dirt was dry, but the fine sand clung to the surface of the barrel. He moved up between the rocks, poked the barrel through the brush.

The Indians came on, sure of themselves. Closing the gap. A hundred and fifty yards. He saw glints of sun from their rifle barrels. Pieces of legs, a blur of moccasin. No bodies. No heads. Heat shimmered off the earth.

Gunn rubbed his eyes. The images were beginning to blur. Yet he couldn't look away. Not for a second.

Two of the ponies were pintos. One was white with a black ring around its eye. The two others were steel gray. Indian ponies. Tough, fast, well-trained. Gunn picked the one he wanted. The one he'd have to bring down with his first shot. The pony had to drop like a stone or his strategy wouldn't work.

The leader was the one with the white horse, the one with its baleful eye ringed in black.

A hundred yards.

Gunn could smell them now.

And, he was sure, they could smell him.

Gunn drew himself to his knees, cocked the rifle, took aim. The cocking sound brought an instant response. It was as if someone had suddenly coughed in a quiet dark room. Then, it was as if everyone in the room struck a match.

Even before he fired, all hell broke loose.

Rifles boomed as smoke from the Winchester blossomed behind a burst of orange flame. Gunn held tight on the white horse's heart, just behind his left front leg. Heart and lung, if he had aimed true, would burst into shredded clouds of blood and meat. The aim was by guess and by gosh. There was no front sight. The Patridge rear sight had been bent from ill use. He aimed more by instinct and practice, almost willing the bullet's trajectory, shooting as if the target were at twenty-five yards instead of just shy of a hundred.

Bullets peppered the earth around him, snapped off twigs. Warriors raced toward him, crouching low, levering bullets and firing as they ran.

The white horse crashed backwards, feet desperately flailing for purchase as the wind was driven from its lungs. The .44 slug mushroomed into a tiny hammer that smashed bone, ripped gristle, tore through the pumping heart, shredded up lung tissue. The Blackfoot leader had to dance lively to avoid the dying animal as it plunged backward, and fell, its legs thrashing in the air.

Despite the charging Indians, the bullets smacking near him, Gunn concentrated his next shot on the leader. The brave weaved towards him in a zig-zag pattern, a war cry ribboning from his lips. Gunn levered quickly, led him four inches and squeezed. The bullet struck the warrior's chest, smashing his breastplate to shards, blowing the air from his lungs. The leader went down, a crimson pool gushing up through a round black hole. His war cry hung in the air for a second, cut halfway in two, then died away like a distant echo swallowed by mountain crevices.

Gunn swung fast, levering another shell into the chamber.

He picked the nearest brave, running headlong toward him at least twenty-five yards. He fired, pointblank. The brave shot backward as if moved by a tremendous invisible force. His hands clutched his belly as his rifle rattled over stone. He pitched headlong into the brush, his entrails gushing from his bowels in a glistening pale blue cord.

The other Indians hit the dirt, disappeared into thin air.

Gunn drew a breath.

Three shells left.

Three Indians. Out there somewhere. Lizards. Snakes. Crawling towards him, quiet as death.

Gunn couldn't move. He had protection where he was. Slight, but some. If he backed out, he would be exposed. If he moved forward, he would be cut down when he tried to stand up.

Stalemate.

Three bullets. Three Indians.

The silence thickened. Stretched into long minutes.

A sound. Hide scraping against sand. A stone

moving slightly, grating against pressure. Something slithering off to his left. A rodent? A serpent? Reptile?

The small sounds became magnified. Deafening.

Gunn reached back, loosened his knife in its sheath. The eagle's head was cold to his touch despite the heat. The bone inlay, smooth. The knife moved easily in its sheath.

It might come to that.

He remembered the words engraved in Spanish on the blade: *No me saques sin razon ni me guardes sin honor.*

Do not draw me without reason, nor keep me without honor.

He had a reason.

Might have.

They came at him then, screaming like banshees. They rose up before him, three hideous wraiths, their cries turning his blood cold.

Bullets sizzled like diving hornets, blew sand and rock into his face. He raised his rifle, shot offhand at the nearest brave. Heard him scream, saw him twist sideways out of the corner of his eye. His rifle was snatched from his hand as a second Indian hurtled at him, headlong.

Gunn felt a hard smack against the side of his head.

Darkness swam before his eyes, fought for domination of his senses.

In the haze, he felt himself drawing his knife. His hand moved slow as if under water. Hot breath steamed his face, his eyes.

Out of the corner of his eye, he saw the fifth brave, charging at him, a gunbarrel pointed straight at his face!

CHAPTER THREE

Gunn brought the knife up hard against the brave who had struck him with his rifle barrel. At the same time, he twisted underneath, falling backward. He dragged the brave with him as his knife slipped up underneath the warrior's ribs. The Indian screamed, squirmed. A shot rang out over Gunn's head.

He slid down the bank. Blood squirted into his hand. His palm, slippery, slipped off the knife handle.

Another shot rang out. The Indian on top of him twitched as the bullet gouged into his spine, deflected upward into his lungs. Shot by his own brother.

Gunn kept sliding, the Indian on top of him a dead weight. He snatched at the rifle barrel still clutched in the brave's hand. His left hand gripped it tightly. His shoulder muscles bulged as he exerted effort to free the rifle from the Indian's grasp. The rifle came free just as Gunn slid into the tepid waters of the St. Regis.

He went under, still holding onto the rifle. The dead brave floated by him, eyes wide and unseeing, hair floating out from his head. The waters turned red with his blood. Gunn felt himself being tugged downstream as the undercurrent swept his legs out from under him. His lungs burned for oxygen. Frantically, he began to kick. His clothes became heavy, waterlogged. The rifle was an anchor in his hand, but he began to paddle with his bloodied right hand, struggling to reach the surface and gulp in air.

Somewhere up there, the other brave waited, his rifle cocked, poised for the kill.

Gunn broke the surface twenty yards downstream.

He propelled himself toward the shore, looking for the other brave on the bank.

The Indian was not there!

He paddled to shore, sogged up on the bank, lay there, panting. He turned the rifle around, poured water out of the barrel. Shook it.

Gunn listened, heard the Indian yelling something.

The horses!

He stood up, climbed to the top of the bank. The lone remaining brave was gathering up the horses, riding a pinto. He had three of them bunched, headed for the road. As Gunn watched, he chased after the fourth. Gunn started running, his water-soaked clothes heavy on his skin. Water flew off as he ran, but he felt as if he was wearing an iron suit.

He couldn't let the Indian take the last horse.

Gunn's feet throbbed with pain as he raced over rocks, through brambles, crashing through brush. The brave had his back to Gunn, was moving away from him at a fast clip. If he didn't act fast, the Indian would be out of range. Gunn stopped, put two fingers in his mouth. He blew on his fingers, emitting an ear-piercing whistle. It was an old trick he had learned when hunting rabbits. A running hare would hear the whistle and stop, curious, making for an easy shot.

Gunn brought the wet rifle up to his shoulder, cocked it. With relief, he heard a shell slide into the chamber.

The Indian jerked on the braided hair reins of his pinto, wheeled.

Just like a jackrabbit.

Gunn brought the barrel down, sighted it just above the brave's head. Range: two hundred fifty yards plus. He squeezed the trigger. The Indian stared at him across the distance. The rifle roared with flame and smoke.

Nothing happened. Hours went by, it seemed.

Then to Gunn's surprise, the Indian raised one hand and fell out of the saddle. Smoke hung in the air, the cordite stinging Gunn's nostrils. With a whoop, he bounded after the pinto which stood there, bewildered, eyeing the fallen brave.

"Whoa boy, steady," Gunn said, making his stalk.

Five minutes later, he was atop the pinto, heading back to the river for his socks, boots, canteen, bedroll and saddlebags.

The other horses followed him for a short

distance, then became interested in eating. Gunn rode on, grim-faced, heading toward Dixon. He had a score to settle and, now that he was mounted, he knew he had a chance.

It was near noon when the tall man rode into Dixon.

People on the street stared at the longlegged Gunn riding bareback on an unshod pinto pony, bedroll draped over the withers, topped by saddlebags, canteen slung from his shoulder, a rifle laid across the saddlebags. An old rifle. No pistol on his hip, his flat-crowned hat pulled low so that people could not see his unshaven face.

Gunn ignored the stares. He was looking for a covered buckboard. Two women.

Dixon was no more than a wide spot in the road, some distance from the St. Regis and the Northern Pacific Railroad. Yet it had the usual: saloons, a hotel, livery stable, barbershop, mercantile store, meat market, some boarding houses, mining and assay offices, law offices and the like. Clark Fork ran by it, fed by the Penn Oreille further north. Ft. Connah and St. Ignatius Mission were the nearest settlements due north at the foot of the Mission Range.

Gunn stopped in front of The Hotel Boston, almost laughed. A false front, two stories, weatherbeaten, it looked more like Alder Gulch than Boston. He tied up the pinto, lugged his gear into the porch, went inside. He had seen no sign of the covered wagon, but vowed to check the livery stable later if he didn't locate the two women before then.

His feet hurt as he stalked through the lobby. Eyes peered over old copies of *The Montana Post* at him. A genteel woman snorted as she looked up from her knitting. The lobby smelled musty, but he also detected the aroma of lye soap and carbolic acid. Someone must have died, or the janitor had given the place its annual scrubbing. The potted plants had at least a quarter inch of dust on the leaves. They stood near the sunlit windows, freshly watered, drooping nonetheless.

The clerk stood behind a rounded counter that jutted into the lobby. Stairs at his left, hallway to the right. He looked up at Gunn as his shadow fell across the counter. He was a man in his early fifties, partially bald, broken nose that had set crooked, tortoise-shell spectacles perched crookedly on a bony ridge above the scar that ran jagged to his left nostril.

"Room," Gunn said.

The clerk pushed a book forward. A pencil rattled across the counter.

"Two dollars."

"Throw in a bath. Hot."

"Fifty cents for the bath. In the back, downstairs. I'll have the woman fill the tub when you're ready."

"I'm ready now." Gunn could smell himself. Smell the painted Indians, the blood, the dank water.

Gunn signed his name, gave the man two dollars and fifty cents. William Gunnison. Saved questions, but he did not use the name much anymore. Not since Laurie died. Part of him had died with her.

"You walk in here?" the clerk asked, handing Gunn a room key.

"Part ways. Why?"

"Lose anything along the way?"

"Some things. You ask a lot of questions, mister." Gunn's pale gray eyes bored into the clerk's.

The clerk bent down behind the counter. He handed Gunn his Winchester, his pistol, and an envelope.

"These yours?" he asked smugly.

Gunn gave him a cold look.

"They are. May I ask how you came by these?"

The clerk avoided his gaze.

"I think you'll find the answer to that inside the envelope the lady left. She said you'd be walking in here in a day or two. I didn't expect you so soon. Hell Gate Canyon's fifty mile from here."

"Yeah." Gunn ripped open the envelope. It reeked of perfume. He pulled out three bills, tens. Thirty dollars. There was a note. Gunn read it slowly.

> *Honorable Sir: We needed your horse. Your arms are hereby returned. The thirty dollars is for your horse. Sorry for any inconvenience.*
>
> *(Miss) Jill Collins*

Oh yeah? Gunn thought. *Thirty dollars for a two hundred dollar horse. And what about my saddle?*

"Is Miss Collins registered here?" he asked the clerk.

"She is, along with her grandmother, Mrs.

Abigail Evanston. Would you care to leave a reply?"

"No, just give me the room number."

"Ah, well," the clerk stammered.

Gunn leaned over the counter, grasped the man's string tie, pulled him close.

"I want to make a personal reply to the ladies," Gunn said evenly. "Now, unless you want me to knock on every door in this fleabag, I'll have that room number, friend."

"Yessir!" the man said quickly. "Three. Two doors down from your room. But they're not in."

Gunn released the clerk, snatched his key up. Room 5. He grabbed his gear, took the stairs to his room three at a time.

An hour later, after a bath and shave, Gunn felt refreshed. His feet felt better, too, after soaking in the hot tub for a half hour. The Chinese woman had given him some balm for his feet. She did laundry, heated the tub water, and both she and her husband worked as maid and handyman for the hotel. He tipped her a dollar, grateful for the balm. He sent her husband out for Climax chewing tobacco, cigars and a bottle of whiskey. The man knocked on Gunn's room soon after Gunn had finished dressing. His name was Hop Chee; his wife's name was Ling.

"Come in, Hop Chee."

"Solly so late. Hop Chee bling mo balm fo' feet."

"Thanks. Mighty considerate. You know the women in number three. Old woman and a young 'un?"

"Me see. Velly pletty gull. Old woman loud mouf."

32

Gunn laughed.

"They come back yet?"

"In loom now. Man follow heah. Him go way. Stlange man."

"A man followed them back from town. When?"

"Just now. Him cally big gun like you gun."

"What's he look like, Hop Chee? Can you describe him?"

"Him not tall, this high." The Chinaman held his hand about four inches over his own head. Hop Chee was small, thin. "Lound hat, baggy pant, clothes dutty, velly dutty. Have cut on face. Ugly face. Little fat."

So the man was on the chunky side, about five foot nine, with a derby, dirty clothes, baggy pants and a scar on his face. A prominent scar.

Gunn gave Hop Chee a tip. The man bowed low several times.

"If you see this man around again, come and tell me, Hop Chee."

"*Dho tze, dho tze,*" he said. "Thank you, thank you."

Gunn wondered why such a man would be following the two women around town. He evidently followed them to the hotel, then left before anyone else saw him. He made a mental note to keep his eyes open for such a man. One thing was sure. He was up to no good. He didn't, evidently, introduce himself to the ladies and he had sneaked behind them all the way from wherever the women had been that morning.

He decided to eat lunch before he called on the women. He needed to build up his strength. He was curious about them. Why had they been in such an all-fired rush to get to Dixon? So rushed that they stole his horse, took his weapons and left him stranded. Yet, they had expected him to show up, obviously. Or had assumed he would. Were they crazy? Both good shots. Tough ladies. But they didn't know the price of a horse such as Buck. Sixteen and a half hands high, the Morgan-Arabian was a special animal. He hadn't paid two hundred for him, but he was worth at least that much to him. Thirty dollars was insulting.

Gunn put the women out of his mind as he walked down to take the pinto to the livery stable. He felt better with the Colt strapped on. It was new, a single action Peacemaker, .45 caliber. Made that year and only a few of them this far west. A drummer had come through Virginia City with half a dozen of them. He hadn't fired twenty rounds through it and yet it was the best pistol he'd ever handled. With its seven-and-one-half-inch barrel, it had a good feel in the hand. The balance was better than any Remington or Starr. Even better, he thought, than a Smith & Wesson. He had a hunch the model would be around a long time. He felt fortunate to own one. Besides, it was a good conversation piece.

He ate a meal of beans, beef and rice, more out of homesickness than anything else. He'd have a steak that night. He didn't want to get sleepy. He still had to see the women, find out what made them tick. And, he either wanted more money for the horse and saddle he had lost, or both returned. He didn't need the money. It was a matter of principle.

He knocked on Room 3.

The door opened.

Gunn wasn't prepared for the beautiful young lady who stood there, one hand behind the door, the other extended in greeting. She wore a bright gingham dress, patent leather shoes, a pearl choker around her neck. Her long black hair was tied back with an orange ribbon. He saw now that she had haunting brown eyes, slightly moist. Her breasts fought for release from the low tight bodice. Her waist was slender, her ankles trim.

"Mr. Gunnison, I presume. We've been expecting you."

"Who's there?" a voice asked testily. Granny.

"You owe me for a saddle," he blurted, "and I'd like my two-hundred dollar horse back." He held out the thirty dollars.

"Come in, Mr. Gunnison," said Jilly in that musical voice that sent shivers up his spine.

She opened the door wider and he saw that her other hand held a small pistol. He recognized it as a Colt Third Model .41. It was silver-plated with pearl handles. The silver plate was scroll engraved, but it was nevertheless, deadly as hell at that range.

Gunn stared at the black holes, over and under, then shifted his gaze to her eyes.

The sparkle had gone away. Her eyes were flat, dark, just like those two muzzles staring at his gut.

"I said come in," she said again. "Or don't you want to?"

CHAPTER FOUR

"I reckon," Gunn said tightly, stepping inside.

Jilly closed the door behind him, locked it. Across the room, on a flowered divan, the grandmother glared at him with hawk eyes.

He turned, not wanting to be shot in the back.

As he stared, the girl reached down and lifted up her skirt, exposing a slender leg and creamy thigh. She slipped the derringer inside a garter holster, her movements slow, provocative. Her eyes softened as she looked up at him, a slow smile beginning to flicker on her lips. She let her dress fall down her leg, a teasing, taunting gesture that was not wasted on Gunn. He smiled broadly at her, a look of admiration on his face.

"Nice little hideout gun," he said quietly. "Nice place to hide it out, too."

"Forgive me," said Jilly, "but when you knocked I wasn't sure who was out there."

"Who were you expecting?"

"Trouble."

Granny rose up from the divan, swept over to them.

"Had you worried, young feller, didn't she?" Granny cackled. "Jilly's a crack shot. Her pappy taught her all he knew and I taught her the rest. Pull up a chair and set a spell. How about some whiskey to wet your whistle?"

Gunn's mouth popped open. Mrs. Evanston was small, but formidable. She chattered like a magpie, spoke like a roughhouse from the St. Louis docks instead of a prim little grandmother all dressed up in crinoline and lace, which she was. She whapped his arm with a folded fan she pulled from her pocket, gestured to a chair. Gunn, bowled over by her energy, stumbled blindly into it.

Jilly laughed and sat next to her grandmother on the divan.

"Now," said the young lady, "I owe you an explanation, Mr. Gunnison."

"Just call me Gunn."

"Why?"

"That's the only name I use. Except on hotel registers."

"We know that," snapped Abigail Evanston. "We wondered if you were the man we'd heard about when we came through Virginia City. We were looking for such a man. You have quite a reputation, young feller. With the ladies, too, I might add."

"You stole my horse, left me without any weapons, ma'am. And five mad Blackfeet."

"We're sorry about that," interjected Jilly. "We thought you were a road agent shooting at us. Or a renegade riding with the Indians."

"That's a hell of a note. Why didn't you ask?"

"Mr. Gunn," said Abigail, "we're two defenseless women and we were all alone out there. Had we known who you were, we would have been more cordial. Now, if you don't mind, while you two talk, I'm going to mix myself a stiff drink. We'll discuss your hurt feelings and your wounded masculine pride a bit later. Jilly, go ahead and tell him why we came to this godforsaken outpost in the middle of nowhere."

"Yes, grandma," the girl said meekly. She leaned back on the divan and crossed her legs. Her skirt slid up her legs slightly. Gunn tried to concentrate on her face instead of her legs. At a sideboard, the granny woman rattled glasses, pouring herself a drink.

Jilly spoke rapidly, her voice rising and falling with emotion. Gunn listened raptly as she told him of her and her grandmother's bizarre quest.

The women had been tracking a scoundrel for months. One Jason Berryman, late of St. Louis. The man presented himself to Jilly as being a wealthy businessman some months before. He wooed her and courted her, sweeping her off her feet. He wedded the young lady in a lavish ceremony that was attended by some of St. Louis' most respectable folk. He paid for the wedding, even though Jilly's family were wealthy. It was unprecedented and she adored him for it. She also trusted him, which had been a sad mistake.

"My grandmother raised me after my parents both died of pneumonia," Jilly explained. "After Jason and I were married, she, as my guardian, arranged for Jason to share a joint bank account."

"A considerable bank account," Abigail cracked wryly as she flounced in a chair next to a table in the large suite.

"Please, Grandmother, don't interrupt."

"Go on, go on, dear. Tell Mr. Gunn the sordid details."

Without consummating the marriage, Jilly explained sadly, Jason withdrew forty thousand dollars in joint funds and disappeared. Pinkerton men, hired by Mrs. Evanston, reported that the man had headed west, presumably for Montana Territory, by rail. He left a trail a mile wide, gambling, whoring, cheating, stealing. They learned that he had married several times before, always leaving the wealthy bride behind, minus savings, dowry, whatever cash they might possess. Most, or all, of the young ladies were too humiliated to complain. But not Jilly. She was determined to find Jason Berryman and get her forty thousand dollars back.

"We almost caught up with him in Union City," said Jilly. "Then, he took the train to Billings. We missed him by a day there. Then, in Virginia City, we thought we had him. But someone tried to kill us there. We asked if there was any man willing enough to go with us and bring Berryman to justice. That's where we heard your name. But Jason had left and, as we discovered, so had you."

"What happened at Hell Gate?" Gunn asked.

"I'll tell you what happened," Granny said, rising

from her chair, waving her glass in the air. "Someone shot both our horses a few miles from there. We saw tracks and followed them on foot. We thought they belonged to the bushwackers who had shot our horses. We found a herd of horses tied up and nobody watchin' 'em, so we took 'em. Hooked 'em to our wagon and were headed for Dixon when all those Injuns come screamin' down out of the hills, all painted and shootin', a bunch of heathens from hell. We turned back toward the canyon when you saw us."

Gunn marveled at Abigail Evanston's speech. At times, she spoke like a refined, upper class St. Louis dowager. But when she was excited, she reverted to the more earthy patois of the farm-raised folk such as he'd grown up with in Arkansas.

In truth, Abigail Evanston, Jilly Collins' maternal grandmother, was a mixture of gentility, Kentucky-bred hill folk shrewdness and nouveau riche veneer that rubbed off at the slightest excuse. Her father had struck it rich in tobacco and then drifted to St. Louis to try his hand at investments that smacked of the future: railroads, real estate, "modern" inventions. She had inherited it all, and lavished her daughter, Honor, with money, prestige, introductions. Jilly's mother had met Roger Collins, a wealthy shipper, sportsman, man-about-town, and they had married. Jill was their only daughter, the inheritor of their wealth. Except their "wealth" had dwindled when unscrupulous partners had drained the estate after her parents' untimely death. Abigail had managed to save some of it, but the forty thousand dollars that Jason Berryman had absconded with was virtually all the money Jill had left. And, Gunn mused wryly, she was still a virgin. She had scarcely been kissed, but she had been screwed royally.

"This Jason Berryman," he said, when the woman had finished telling him the saga of the thief who had stolen both her heart and her money, "what does he look like? Is he a short, heavy man, ugly, with a scar on his face? Wear a derby hat?"

The two women looked at him as if he had just puddled on their floor.

"Jason Berryman?" they said in unison.

Gunn already knew the answer. He just wanted to see if the description he had given the women would spark any recognition.

"Jason is a very handsome scalawag," Abigail said. "Devilishly handsome. He's tall, thin, dark, utterly without conscience, utterly beneath contempt. I'd like to . . ."

"Grandmother!" Jilly warned.

Granny swigged the rest of her drink, pouted. She was ready to blow off steam, but Jill, Gunn gathered, kept reminding her of her position in life. He wondered what the St. Louis rich bitches would think if they'd seen her throwing down on him with a fifty caliber Sharps after holding off a pack of redskins as well as any mountain man.

"Perhaps Mr. Gunn would like to take supper with us, my dear, and listen to our proposition."

"I'd like that very much," he said, feeling that, for the moment, he was being dismissed. "I would also like to talk to you about my horse and saddle."

"In due time, young man, in due time." Granny

lurched from her chair and headed for the sidebar to pour herself another whiskey. Gunn knew it was time to leave.

"It'll put her to sleep," Jilly whispered. "Please forgive her. We'll talk tonight. Call for us about seven?"

"I will, Miss Collins," he said. "With pleasure."

She blew him a naughty kiss as she opened the door.

"Call me Jilly, please. Gunn. I like your name. It fits you."

The Golden Bull was Dixon's best restaurant, such as it was. It was run by an amiable couple who had migrated west from Kansas City, developed food poisoning almost everywhere they ate and decided that Dixon was the place to found an eating place. In season, they featured elk and antelope, venison and trout. They also bought beef from the same suppliers who sold to the Army and, although some said the meat sometimes tasted sweet, like horsemeat, the Skinners denied using old Dobbin when beef was in short supply. Ed waited tables, Josie did the cooking, but sometimes they traded off. Ed was a better cook, but he liked to meet people and Josie preferred to stay back in the kitchen and dream of opening a fine restaurant in San Francisco.

". . . So now we figger Jason's headed for Idyho," Granny was saying in her best cracker accent, after consuming almost an entire jug of elderberry wine with her beefsteak. "He knows we're a-breathing down his neck, a-buggin' out his underwear!''

"Granny!" Jilly chided, no longer trying to continue the pretense about her grandmother. They'd had some whiskeys before supper, wine with the meal and now the table was glistening with snifters of brandys—all on Abigail Evanston. She had insisted.

"The point is, Gunn," Jilly said, her eyes glittering from the candlelight and the wine and the brandy, "we need a man's thinking. Jason is too quick for us. We think we're smarter than he is in some things, but he always seems to know when we're getting close."

"Maybe," Gunn said quietly, "he knows you're coming because he has extra eyes."

"Huh?" said Jilly.

"What's that, young feller?"

Gunn leaned across the table, drew his fingers together in a wedge. His lower lip was kinked as he raked a tooth along its edge. His powerful shoulders made his upper torso look massive in the dim light. The other diners had long since gone. The Skinners were catching up on the dishes, leaving the trio alone. Every so often, Ed would peer through the double doors to see if the diners needed anything.

"I mean, suppose Jason has paid spies to follow you wherever you are. This afternoon I asked you if Jason looked like a certain squat, ugly individual in a bowler hat. You missed the point. The reason I asked was that such a man was seen following you. Here, in Dixon."

The women exchanged glances, protested until

Gunn had to wave them down.

"All right, all right. You didn't see him. But he knows you're here. He's interested in you. What if Berryman paid this jasper to watch you two and report to him when you got into a town and when you left? Hell, you'd never catch him."

Jilly sucked in her breath.

Granny made an obscene noise with her lips.

Jilly looked thoughtful.

"You know," she said, "you just may be right. I've been wondering how Jason always manages to stay one step ahead of us."

"The question remains, Mr. Gunn," said Abigail, trying once again to assume command over her speech, "will you accompany us to Idaho? We wish to leave in the morning. We will return your horse, pay for your saddle. In addition, we will pay you a fee for helping us recover the money owed my granddaughter by Jason Berryman. Say, five percent?"

Gunn's jaw tightened. A muscle in his cheek spasmed. He shoved his brandy glass toward the center of the table. He gave Abigail a hard look, his pale eyes smoky with smouldering feelings deep inside him.

He looked at Jilly. She was beautiful in the lamplight. He saw the pleading in her eyes. She was desperate, facing things she didn't understand, trying to hold her own in a rough land, a land dominated by men. She had guts. He would give her that. He admired her for it. But she was in way over her head. Men like Berrymen were thick as fleas on a hound's ear out in the West. They preyed on women, on other men, feeding on their weaknesses, their greed, their gullibility. He hated to see her suffer so, but it was really none of his business. Berryman would eventually come to the end of his string. His kind always did. He wondered if Jilly wanted to get her money back or if she just wanted revenge. A woman scorned—was a dangerous woman indeed.

"I'll lay it out straight for you ladies," Gunn said, his voiced pitched low. "I have no doubt you've been wronged, Miss Collins. Jilly. And I know you're facing a long hard trail, chasing after this scoundrel. But you made your choice and it's your fight. Not mine. But that's not the reason I won't go with you after Berryman. In fact, I'm heading the same way, to Idaho, eventually. I'm in no hurry. The reason I won't side with you in this is that my gun isn't for hire. I believe a man who lives by the gun, dies by the gun. Thanks for your offer, but I am not a bounty hunter. I don't hunt men for pay, nor anything else, for that matter."

Jilly reacted as if he'd slapped her. Disappointment showed in her eyes. She dipped them, veiled them under long dark lashes.

Abigail's lips tightened. She glared at Gunn, her feelings boiling up inside her.

"I submit, Mr. Gunn, or Gunnison, whatever your name is, that you are without heart. You have crushed my granddaughter's hopes, and mine as well. Beyond that, Mr. Gunn, I say you are an out and out coward. I don't know how you gained your reputation as a man who is not afraid to use his gun when it is needed, but I'd say that such a reputation

45

is not merely overblown, but patently false."

Gunn tossed his napkin onto the table, shoved his chair away from it and stood up.

"Come on, ladies," he said sadly, "I'll walk you home and bid you goodnight. Thank you for a most interesting evening."

Abigail Evanston extracted a wad of bills from her purse, flung them on the table. She grabbed Jilly's arm and led her out the door as Gunn stood there, dumbfounded.

Seconds later, a shot rang out. He heard a cry of pain and a woman scream in terror.

CHAPTER FIVE

Gunn rushed outside, drawing his pistol.

His first thought was that someone had shot Jilly Collins.

The moment his silhouette was framed in the doorway another shot boomed in the night. The door shuddered as the slug hit it. Splinters tugged at his vest, spattered against his hat. He saw the orange flame from across the street, the quick illumination of a man's form between two silent dark buildings.

Gunn crouched and angled left out of the lighted doorway. Behind him he heard the Skinners babbling frantically over the disturbance.

Abigail lay on the porch, Jilly squatting next to her, crying with concern. He saw them only out of the corner of his eye.

"You hurt?" he whispered to Jilly.

"Grandmother. She was shot."

"Keep down."

Gunn heard footsteps retreating between the two buildings. He couldn't see anything. He raced across the street, zigzagging, hunching low.

He saw the man briefly, just before he disappeared in back of the buildings. The man ran to his left, Gunn after him.

Briefly, he saw the Skinners come out of the restaurant to give assistance to Mrs. Evanston.

Then he moved between the buildings, pistol in hand, listening. He knew that he could catch a lead ball at any time. It was pitch dark, quiet, as he emerged behind the buildings. A narrow alley, the backs of buildings looming up over him. The scrape of a boot to his left. He dashed to the other side of the alley.

A shot crashed, almost in his ear. The whine of the bullet sizzled past his ear, smashed into a stack of oaken barrels behind him. The impression of the orange flame lingered on his vision. Twenty feet away, behind some crates, the ambusher waited. Gunn backed into the shadows, careful to make no sound. A step. Another. He reached the stacked barrels, slid behind them. Somehow, he had to draw the shooter out in the open. Make him commit himself one more time.

Gunn stook on tiptoe, reached upward with his left arm. His palm touched the stave of a barrel. He pushed, then ran around the side. The barrel tumbled from its perch, rolled into the alley. It rumbled toward the back of a building.

The man stood, fired twice.

The barrel splintered under the shock of the driven lead, shattered, twisted sideways.

Gunn shot at the flash, centering his aim in the barely visible outlines of the man, a touch below the afterglow of the flaming pistol.

He heard a loud click as the gunman's hammer and firing pin smacked into an empty chamber.

A loud *whoof!*

Gunn rushed forward, cocking his single action. The man reeled, staggered towards him, trying vainly to lift his gun. His empty gun. Behind him, two doors down, a lamp glowed through a window. Gunn saw the man's silhouette clearly now. The derby hat.

"Drop it," he said, crouching in case the man's pistol had only misfired. "Drop it or I'll take your head off."

"Uuuuuuurrrrrrrhhhhh!" the man groaned, dropping his pistol. He swayed there in the alley, as if bewildered, confused. Gunn walked the half dozen feet remaining and turned the man around to face the dim light. The scar was livid across his cheek. The same man Hop Chee had told him about.

He was hurt bad. Gunn saw the spreading stain of dark in the man's groin, just below his belt.

He dragged the would-be assassin down to the light, stretched him out. The man looked at him with waxen eyes. There was a trickle of blood seeping out of the corner of his mouth. The shock of the bullet's impact had caused him to bite his tongue. His tongue hung out of the other side of his mouth, sawed halfway in two.

Gunn knelt beside him. He rammed the barrel of his pistol into the side of the man's throat.

"You don't have much time, feller. Why'd you

shoot the old woman?"

"You shot me."

Gunn nodded. He moved the barrel of his pistol up so the man could see it. Held it two inches from his eyes. Maybe that would help the man to recover his senses.

"I want a name. Yours, the man who hired you."

"God, it hurts. Pete. Pete Scaggs."

"Who? The man who paid you to shoot the woman?"

"My name. Pete Scaggs." The words were garbled, but Gunn understood him. The man didn't know he had bitten his tongue. He spoke as if he had a chunk of raw meat between his teeth. "Jason Berryman paid me."

"Look, Scaggs, if I get you to a sawbones, he maybe can get that bullet out and sew you back up. But I want to know everything Berryman told you, how much he paid you. You haven't got a hell of a lot of time."

"Hard to talk. Berryman gave me five hunnert. Wanted me to kill the old woman. Said if I didn't, he had another feller here to kill me."

"Who?"

"Didn't say. Get me that doc, mister. I feel real bad."

Gunn looked down at the man's wound. The bullet had hit him low, but he could already smell the stench of split intestines. The man was being poisoned, probably wouldn't make it even if a surgeon could get the bullet out. It was like a horn wound. There were so damn many things severed, broken, smashed, cut, pulped, that it would take a miracle to keep the man alive.

"Where's Berryman now?"

"Gone. Day before yestidy."

"Where?"

"West. The Mission, I reckon."

"I'll get you a doc. Hold on." Gunn fished in the man's pockets, took out a wad of money. "I'll give this back to the owner," he said.

Gunn stood up, walked to the back door of the place where the lamp shone through the window. He banged on the back door. No answer. People inside were probably scared out of their wits. All that gunfire. He heard voices on the street. Quickly he holstered his gun, walked swiftly between the buildings, back over to the Golden Bull.

A crowd stood where Abigail and Jilly had been. The doors to the restaurant were open. Gunn's heart sank. If the old woman was dead . . .

He shouldered his way through the crowd, went inside.

Abigail was sitting on a chair, happily chattering away, sipping brandy. Jilly beamed when she saw Gunn.

"Grandmother's all right. The bullet just grazed her."

A man in a dark suit stood next to the Skinners, closing a small canvas satchel.

"You the doc?"

"I am."

"Man in the alley across the street. Shot in the gut. Can you help him?"

"I think so. You shoot him?"

"In self-defense. He shot this woman, Mrs.

Evanston. She going to be all right?"

"Her pride was hurt more than anything," said the doctor, who looked as if he practiced boozing more than medicine. He had a three-day beard, reeked of cheap whiskey. Yet he wasn't drunk. Just jovial. He smiled at Gunn indulgently. Actually, Percy Merriwether was the barber, druggist and physician. He acted, as many barbers did in those days, as a surgeon. He was good at cutting and bandaging. And he was no stranger to his own anesthetic—alcohol, which he used liberally, both externally and internally.

"Mrs. Evanston sustained a flesh wound in her arm. I've given her powders. She should get some rest for a few days."

"And all the whiskey I want?" asked Abigail.

"It won't hurt you none," said Merriwether.

"Doc, if you don't get on back there, you'll be prescribing candles and crepe. Skinner, better get the sheriff, if you got one. The man's name is Pete Scaggs and he shot Mrs. Evanston."

Gunn managed, with Jilly's help, to get Abigail back to the hotel and in her bed. She played the role of injured dowager to the hilt, insisting that neither of them make a fuss over her. All she wanted, she said, was a nightcap. More whiskey. This was done.

"You have your hands full," Gunn told Jilly. "I'll say good night."

"Must you leave now?"

"I think it's better. She's liable to wake up. Complain. I'll see you in the morning. I'll go after Jason Berryman now. Any man who would hire another to shoot a nice old lady like that deserves to be caught up short. No money, though. If it's ever mentioned again, I ride on. Leave you flat."

"I understand."

"Goodnight, Jilly."

"Goodnight, Gunn." Her words lingered in his ears long after he had gone out the door, walked to his own room. He couldn't figure her out. She was as changeable as a chameleon's color. She was beautiful, desirable, yet she seemed to be controlled by her grandmother. It wasn't uncommon. She was a virgin, born of wealthy parents. She had qualities that he admired. He liked the way she handled a gun. Her fearlessness, her determination. No man could step on her. She had been hoodwinked, but she hadn't let it pass. She was going after the man. She meant to bring him to justice—her justice. Put him out of business. That was something in his book. Still, she puzzled him. He had never met any woman like her. She was soft, feminine, yet she had a hard core to her that belied her youth. Product, he supposed, of her upbringing—a strong father, perhaps a strong mother as well. Good pioneer stock. Salt of the earth.

When he got in bed, he was still thinking of her.

The Indians all rode little gray canvas bags that kept spilling candles and bandages all over the battlefield. The Indians had white skin, alabaster white, and painted bellies. The paint squirmed like red worms as they rode toward him. The Indians' faces kept changing. There was Scaggs and Jilly and Abigail, Josie Skinner, the hotel clerk, the doc, and finally, one whose face was like a black thundercloud. Lightning shot out of the cloud and thunder boomed. He felt himself being snatched up out of a river, his feet as large as snowshoes and blood red. A faceless man held him by the throat and kept pounding his head against the rock wall of a canyon. Every time his head hit the rock, the lightning crashed. The thunder boomed, boomed, boomed, boomed.

Gunn sat up, wild-eyed, his eyes gripping the side of his head.

For several seconds he couldn't figure out where he was.

Then, gradually, his head began to clear. The knock sounded again. Knock knock knock knock.

Someone was at the door!

"Who is it?" he called softly, his hand reaching through the dark for his pistol, snug under his pillow.

"Jilly," came the loud whisper.

Jilly!

Groggy with the drugs of sleep, Gunn rose from the bed, opened the door a crack.

"What's the matter?"

"Let me in."

She whispered into the room wearing only a light wrap over her diaphanous gown. Moonlight, seeping through the window, bathed her in silver. Gunn sucked in his breath. He want to the dresser, fumbled for sulphur matches.

"No, don't light the lamp."

"Huh? What do you want, Jilly?" He turned to face her.

She came to him, put a soft finger against his lips. Silk material rubbed against his legs. He wore only shorts; realized he was near naked. She pressed him against the dresser, her hands moving up his sides, spidery, tingling. He felt her body nestle against him. Felt his manhood stir as strange sensations shot through his flesh.

"Jilly?"

"Uh?"

"You sure you know what you're doing?"

"I know," she breathed.

Her arms twined around his neck. Hands pulled his head down. She stood on tiptoes, kissed him. She made a purring kitten sound in her throat, half-growl, half-mew as her lips touched his. Her tongue slithered into his mouth, sending a shock of electricity through him. He dropped his arms around her, drew her close. Close enough so that he felt the contours of her body meld to his.

"I got cheated once," she husked. "I don't want to be cheated again."

One of her hands fell to his hip, grasped it urgently. He felt her hand tug at him, tug at his shorts. He kissed her hard on the mouth, overcome by a sudden desire of his own. She smelled fresh as if she had bathed and powdered. As if she had dabbed perfume behind her ears, under her breasts.

"You don't want this, Jilly," he said quietly. "I'm no St. Louis man. No gentleman."

"I want you, Gunn, I know that. That's all that matters. Not who we are. Or were."

Her hand went inside his shorts, found his growing manhood. Squeezed. Fire shot through his loins.

He twisted into her, drew her up to him again. Kissed her brutally. She didn't retreat. His hands pulled her wrap from her shoulders. He looked down at young breasts fighting to flow out of the nightgown's bodice. He touched them through the material, felt her body tauten.

He carried her to the bed, slipped out of his shorts as she tussled with her gown. She tossed it into the air. It floated to the floor like a delicate moonstruck shadow.

"Why?" he said, as he slid in beside her on the bed.

"I have to find out something. I'll tell you later."

"That may be too late. You can't go back, you know. You won't be the same."

"No. Hush up. Kiss me. Love me."

Her breath came quick when he kissed her breast. He fed on her like some grazing animal, first one nipple, then the other. He felt her body contract and relax, felt her squirm with pleasure as his mouth roamed over the soft mounds, his tongue lapping at the hardening buds. She said things that he couldn't hear, words he couldn't understand They were not words, but throat sounds that made his manhood stand drumtight. He slid up to her face, kissed her lips, a suddenly hungered man.

"Good lord," she breathed. "You set me on fire. All over. All through me."

He knew what she meant. A moment later, her hand found him. Pulled on his stalk, squeezed it. Squeezed it again and again as if the fingers themselves were unbelieving, unsure of its reality. He caressed her gently between her legs, pressing on the soft folds of her sex, fingering the sheath, tracing a path along the velvety inner lining. Her touch became more urgent. Her fingers tightened their grasp. He slid atop her, forced her legs apart until she understood.

His hands gripped her buttocks. He drew her up to him as he entered her. He moved downward, slipping his hardness inside her. She gasped with pleasure, clawed at him with desparate hands. He felt the barrier of her maidenhead, pushed hard against it, retreated. Again. As she breathed in the room's silence, in the silence of the moonlight filtering through the window like pale silver gauze.

"Go on," she said. "Break it."

"I don't want to hurt you."

"It hurts more having it."

He lunged at her. Hard. Down. Thrusting like a battering ram. The leathery shield ripped asunder, parted with the force of his plunge. She cried a quick short cry, then surged to him as he sank his swollen cock clear to the mouth of her womb. Her eyes misted, her hips ground into his. She sighed as her body shuddered with the first wavelet of orgasm.

He took her then, savagely. The wavelets surged to gigantic tides. Her body rocked with his, bucked beneath him, thrashed with climax after climax. Mindlessly, he bored into her as her hands raked his back, fingers digging into him with every eruption of joy in her being.

His own climax came, jolting him back from the high dark sky where he had been. For a time he had imagined he had been with Laurie. Laurie, so young, like this, so pliant, yielding, giving, wanting, needing. But it was Jilly and he knew it was she because she was weeping and laughing, kissing him frantically, thanking him as he drained his seed into her and went limp and fell away from her like some feeble drowned man washed to shore after fighting a raging sea for hours, days, years.

CHAPTER SIX

They lay there in silence for a long time.

He breathed, feeling his strength returning. He sniffed the aroma of sweat and perfume, of bath powder and the mingled musk of their loins. Her hand lay on his flat belly as if she needed that contact to assure herself that he was still there. He turned his head, looked at her. He saw her face, not her eyes. Those were lost in shadow, but he sensed their peering forces. He sensed her smile, gradually determined its shape.

There was an emptiness afterwards. Now. Shreds of memory intruded on his thoughts. He saw Laurie in the half-dark, but the smell was not Laurie. The dark fan of hair on the pillow was not Laurie. The delicate nymph form was not Laurie. But, almost. He had thought she would go away. And she did, most of the time. She stayed away, until he lay with a woman like this. And then she came back, parts of her. The good parts he remembered. Wanted.

His eyes closed like fists. He turned away from Jilly.

"What's the matter?"

"Nothing," he said.

"You—you made me very happy. I didn't know it would be like this."

Like what?

Laurie had said something like that. The first time. He couldn't remember her exact words. Just her intonation. Like Jilly's words. Full of wonder. Full of awe.

"I—I want you again, Gunn. Is that terrible of me?"

"No. Natural, I'd say."

She sat up, an eager child. Her long black hair flowed over her shoulders like a shawl.

"Really? Do people do it a lot? I mean, a man and a woman? More than once a night?"

Gunn laughed deep in his chest.

"Yeah, I reckon. If it's good."

"It was good wasn't it? For you? It was for me. More than good. Best. Better than anything."

"It was good." He folded his hands behind his head, his arms making triangles. Looked up at her. Her breasts were small, pert, upturned. Cute. Like baby quail. She was someone to marvel at, full of contradictions, full of budding womanhood. He knew little about her, yet she was made of solid substance. She had depths yet unplumbed, mysteries not yet revealed. Their paths had crossed and neither of them could tell where it all would lead. She was someone to watch, to think about, to love, perhaps, for as long as they were together on the unknown trail.

"Gunn?"

"Yeah?"

"You know I hated you when I first saw you."

"It looked that way to me."

"No, not back at the canyon. I didn't know you then. I was scared. Thought you were in cahoots with Jason. I mean when I first saw you here, in the hotel. After I knew who you were. Jason did that to me. He made me mistrust all men. Made me see them all in his light."

"And now?"

"Now I realize I was wrong. There are good men. And bad." Her hand began rubbing his belly, scribing aimless circles on his flesh. "You protected me, risked your life out there. I know you did it because you were, are, a good man. Now you say you'll help us go after Jason. I'm glad. I want you to help. I can't do it alone."

"You're going after him in the morning?"

"Yes. Grandmother can join us later. She needs rest."

"And my horse?"

"You'll have it back. A new saddle, too."

"Blackmail," he teased.

"No, not any more." She climbed on him, then, straddling his torso with slim pulsing legs. He reached up, cupped her breasts, kneaded them like dough. She squirmed, finding him with her sex, her black wiry thatch rubbing his manhood until it responded, hardening with engorged blood.

He took her, then, surprising her with his upward

thrust, his quick entry.

They made love several times, until dawn spread a pale light over their sated bodies, then gilded them with sun.

The knock came a half hour after Jilly had gone back to her room.

Gunn was dressed, his pistol strapped on. He opened the door.

Percival Merriwether stood there with another man. The other man wore a badge.

"May we come in?" The doc looked as if he had been up all night, but he had shaved. He smelled of bay rum and stale whiskey. "This is our sheriff, Deke Naylor."

Gunn let them in, regarded the lawman.

Deke Naylor was past fifty, with graying sideburns, bowed legs, barrel chest. He was about five feet eight inches tall, wore miners' boots, a low crowned hat that had all but lost its shape. His face was windburned, blue-veined, with close-set hazel eyes, a scarred red nose. His belly hung over his gunbelt. Part of his undershirt showed where a button had popped off from the sheer weight of his gut.

"Gunnison? You the one that had that run-in with Bull Roumal over to Virginia City last year?"

Gunn nodded.

Naylor stretched out a bony hand, a hand that was weather cracked, splotched with brown spots.

"Like to hear your version of what happened last night." Gunn waved the men to chairs, sat on the edge of the rumpled bed. He told them of hearing

62

the shot, of chasing Pete Scaggs to the alley, of shooting him.

"I told the doc to take care of him, brought the women back to the hotel."

Merriwether and Naylor exchanged glances.

"Mind if I take a look at that knife you got on your gunbelt, Mister Gunnison?"

"What for?" Gunn was wary.

"Nice lookin' knife."

Gunn slipped the knife from its sheath, handed it butt-first to the sheriff.

Naylor turned the blade over in his hands, read the legend, which he didn't understand. He sniffed the knife, ran a hand down the blade.

"Ain't been newly oiled. Don't smell of blood."

Merriwether nodded, shrugged. Naylor handed the knife back to Gunn.

"What's this all about?" he asked.

Merriwether cleared his throat.

"Go ahead, Percy, tell him," said the sheriff.

"I went over to the alley, found the man you shot like you said. Only trouble was, he was dead."

"Funny. I thought he'd make it if he got his guts sewn back together." Gunn looked puzzled.

"Oh, it wasn't the gunshot wound that killed him," said Merriwether. "His throat was slit. Ear to ear."

Gunn waited for Jilly. Buck stamped his foot impatiently. The new saddle creaked every time the horse moved. He had spent the better part of an hour working neat's foot oil into the leather. It was a good saddle, but he wished he still had his old one. Some pilgrim would pick it up, sell it for twenty dollars or so. He had Jilly's horse too, saddled and ready.

Where in hell was that girl?

It was late afternoon. After the doc and the sheriff had left, he had gone to see Jilly and her grandmother. He told them it was important that they leave Dixon as soon as possible. The sheriff would arrange to have a man keep an eye on Mrs. Evanston. But Gunn thought it was better if Jilly and he weren't seen together in town.

When he had talked to Scaggs, the man had said Jason Berryman would kill him if he failed in his mission to stop Jilly Collins and her grandmother.

And that's exactly what had happened.

Someone had been watching. Someone had slipped into the alley and put a knife to Pete's throat. Just as Berryman had promised.

So, there was another assassin in Dixon.

But who?

Gunn tried to picture the kind of man he was looking for. He would be someone you'd not notice particularly. A sneak. A damned footpad, most likely. Every town in the West had its share. These were the sneak thieves who worked best at night. Robbing, raping, killing. The man would be a skulker, someone who knew how to slip through town unnoticed. For the first time since he had heard about Jason Berryman, Gunn began to wonder what kind of a man would bilk a young woman out of money and then pay others to have her killed. Berryman's heart must be as black as the ace of spades. He was beginning to feel hatred for him, the kind of hatred he had felt for Jason Coker in Colorado and Bull Roumal in Bannack. Such men didn't deserve to live.

He had told Jilly to sneak out of the hotel, meet him out back. He didn't want her walking down Main Street. From the doc's description of the wound in Pete Scagg's throat, the footpad was pretty fancy with a knife. The wound was clean, almost surgical. The way the doc told it, whoever did it for Scaggs held his head back and sliced a neat second smile under his chin. The cut was deep enough to kill; the knife was as sharp as a razor.

Gunn stood in the shadows of an outbuilding. He rolled a quirly. He was getting nervous. Jilly should have been there by now. The plan was for Abigail to stay in Dixon for four or five days, then sell the wagon, take the supply stage to Mission Cataldo. He and Jilly could travel faster by horseback. The Rawlings Freight Company ran a line from Spokane to Missoula and had other lines to the outback settlements in the territory. Abigail would be all right. The sheriff would see that she had an escort to the mission settlement.

Gunn saw some boys pitching horseshoes in the next block. Every time he heard a shoe ring on the iron stob, he winced. The boys were drinking, or had been, and made a lot of noise. Smoke from an outdoor cookfire drifted his way. Clothes were hanging on the lines behind the scattered houses back of the alley, flapping in the breeze. The wind had cooled things down, but the sun shone bright as a copper penny. It was a good day to leave, to get on the trail. He lit the cigarette, drew the dry smoke into his lungs.

Hop Chee came out the back door of the hotel. He carried a bunch of wet towels. He saw Gunn and grinned widely. He walked to the line, hung up the towels. He wore the loose silky clothes of the Chinese, sandals, a small beanie on his head. He grinned at Gunn all the time he was hanging the towels up.

Buck tried to nip Jilly's horse in the neck. Gunn jerked the reins, spoke sharply to the animal.

Hop Chee grinned.

"You take lide?" he called over.

Gunn nodded.

"You go pletty gull?"

"Yeah. You seen her? Miss Collins?"

"Hop Chee no see. Go fetch."

The Chinaman finished draping the soggy towels on the line, shuffled on sandaled feet back to the hotel's rear entrance. Gunn watched him carelessly. Hop Chee stooped slightly forward, his loose camisole hanging out in front, tight in the back. There was an odd outline of something in the rear of the man's waistband. It looked like a stick. Probably what he used to stir the towels in the vat when he washed them out.

The Chinaman's sandals clattered on the porch.

He turned, bowed to Gunn, and grinned again.

Gunn waved him on, tired of the obsequious mannerisms of the man. Still, he owed him something. He had been the one to tell him about Scaggs. He had meant to thank him, but hadn't. Everyone in town knew of the shooting now. And they knew, too, that someone had cut Scagg's throat. It was funny that Hop Chee hadn't mentioned it. After all, he'd warned Gunn that Scaggs was following the women.

Something ticked in Gunn's brain. Clawed at it for recognition. Something he couldn't quite grasp. It was there, he just couldn't get it.

Hop Chee opened the back door, went inside.

A horseshoe rang on the iron post. A cheer from the boys floated to him. The towels flapped on the line, dripped water on the ground. Jilly's horse raked a shod hoof in the dirt. Buck flicked his tail impatiently.

Gunn's mind went back to Hop Chee. That odd outline he had seen through the camisole.

Then to Scaggs.

The doc's explanation of the knife wound.

Someone sneaky. A footpad. Someone no one would notice. Someone who was so much a part of the town no one would pay much attention to him. Someone who knew that Scaggs had failed and had to die.

The thought in Gunn's mind took shape. A light came on in his skull.

Hop Chee!

Why hadn't he seen it before? The women had said they'd seen no one following them. That was because no one was following them. Scaggs didn't need to follow them. He knew their movements from the time they had come in to Dixon. He knew where they had dined, waited for them to leave. He picked his moment because he knew! Someone had told him.

Someone who knew every move the two women made.

Because he was there! Close. In the hotel!

Hop Chee.

Gunn tossed the quirly down, ground it out with his bootheel. Quickly, he tied the reins of the two horses to one of the posts on the clothesline. He raced toward the hotel.

Jilly was in danger.

Hop Chee might be waiting for her in the dark hallway. Or, he might be knocking on the door of her room right at that moment.

The outline he'd seen in the waistband could only be one thing.

A knife.

A very sharp knife. The same one that had cut Scaggs' throat.

Fear rose up in Gunn's throat.

He prayed he wouldn't be too late!

CHAPTER SEVEN

Jilly glanced at herself one more time in the mirror. She tucked a stray wisp of hair up under her wide-brimmed hat. She wore riding clothes, loose enough for comfort, trim enough to show her girlish curves to advantage, and only a small amount of makeup, a slight touch of rouge rubbed into her cheeks, a tiny amount on her lips.

"You be careful, hear?" Abigail ordered from her bed. "I'll be along directly."

"I know, Grandmother. Please, I can take care of myself."

Abigail's left arm was bandaged, in a sling. She made sure that it was highly visible as she sat propped up in bed. At her bedside there was a pistol, also prominently displayed. She had the fierce look of a wounded hawk. A bottle of whiskey was handy, powders for the pain. But there was no pain. Just a dull ache where the bullet had furrowed through the fleshy part of her arm. If Jilly hadn't been on the other side of her and a step ahead, she might have been killed.

"Stayin' out all night, with that man. I'm ashamed of you, Jilly."

But she wasn't. She was proud. She liked Gunn. Trusted him. She sized up men quickly. And women. Jilly was a good girl. She had probably needed what Gunn had given her. Lord knows, she had been terribly disappointed, not to mention humiliated, after the truth came out about Jason Berryman. Of course Gunnison was beneath her station. She could never marry such a man. But she had never seen her granddaughter bloom so! Had they just "talked" as Jilly said? She didn't believe it for a moment. She knew how a woman looked when a man had made love to her. That was the way Jilly looked this morning. And now.

"I'm ready," Jilly announced. "Do what the doctor says, Grandmother. That was nice of him to stop in and change your dressing."

"A lot of fuss over nothing!" Abigail snorted.

"Oh, you love it!"

Jilly went over to her grandmother, kissed her on the cheek. Her eyes misted. So did Abigail's.

"You go on, now, girl. That man's probably having a conniption waiting this long for you. Go on!"

"Goodbye, Grandmother. Please be good."

"You be good. Or if you can't, then be careful."

Jilly blushed. She hefted her leather bag off the table. Her hideout pistol and female things were inside. She wore the Starr on her hip, visible. She waved at Abigail as she let herself out. "Lock this door!" she called.

Quickly, she walked down the hall.

The desk clerk looked up, startled, as she passed by. The sheriff's deputy, sitting in the lobby, looked up from his newspaper. When he saw who it was, he got up, followed Jilly. She paid him no attention, but went around the front desk and down the hall. The hall was dark. She smelled soap from the bathroom at the end. The door was open. The deputy paused, watched her walk on. He would go back to his seat when he heard the back door slam. He knew Gunn was waiting for her out back.

"Sssst!"

Jilly stopped.

Ling, Hop Chee's wife, stood in the doorway, hissing at her. The Chinese woman beckoned to Jilly with her finger.

"What is it, Ling?"

"You come first. Heah."

Jilly followed Ling into the tub room.

Ling closed the door behind her. Jilly heard the key turn in the lock.

Before she knew what was happening, Ling had pulled the Starr from its holster.

"Wha—" she started.

Then, strong hands gripped her arms, drew them back of her. She half-turned, saw the hard frozen mask of Hop Chee's face over her shoulder.

There was a rapid singsong dialogue in Chinese, low, offkey, but oddly musical.

Hop Chee shoved Jilly forward, toward the oaken tub. Ling danced just ahead, hopping from side to side in that peculiar gait of the Chinese.

In horror, Jilly saw that the tub was full.

71

Before she could respond, she saw Ling reach up for her, knock her hat off. Then, Ling's hands grabbed her hair, pulled her head down toward the water. She opened her mouth to scream. Ling shoved her face into the water.

Suddenly, Jilly realized what they were going to do. Her blood turned to ice.

They were going to drown her.

The deputy saw Jilly go into the tub room. He stood there at the end of the hall, waiting. Deke had told him to keep an eye on the women in the hotel, follow either of them if they went out. He knew the girl was leaving with Gunnison and then he would only have the granny to worry about. Idly, he wondered why she had gone into the tub room. Why had he heard a *click*, as if someone had locked the door?

Locked the door!

Deputy Sheriff Fred Hall blinked his eyes. The whole picture had not dawned on him yet. Then, before he could move, the back door opened, slammed with a crash. There, bounding towards him was the big man, Gunn.

Something about Gunn's manner made Hall realize that he had made a mistake. A serious mistake. Hall recovered quickly as Gunn raced toward him.

"Jilly!" Gunn shouted. "Where is she? Where's the Chinaman?"

"Jesus," exclaimed Hall. "The Collins lady went in the wash room. Door's locked."

"You dumb bastard!"

72

Gunn whirled quickly, ran to the door. It was, as the deputy had said, locked. He put pressure against it. There was no sound from inside.

"Jilly!"

Sounds. Scraping sounds.

In a flash, Gunn could see Jilly's beautiful throat laid open, a knife sawing across it. Enraged by the image, he backed away from the door, ran at it, his shoulder dropped low. The deputy drew his pistol. The door gave with a splintering wrench as Gunn's one hundred and ninety pounds smashed into it.

Ling and Hop Chee stood on either side of Jilly. They looked at the charging Gunn with blank faces, glittering eyes. They had her head in the tub, under water. Jilly hung there, limp. Lifeless. Ling swung one arm free. Her hand held the Starr pistol. She started to pull the trigger. The pistol was self-cocking, a double action, first issued in 1860. But the trigger pull was too strong for the frail Chinese woman. Gunn was on her in a split second, wresting the pistol from her grasp.

She cursed him in rapid Chinese, dockworker Cantonese, *"Kyow dzing-e, pyow dzing-e!"*

Gunn slapped her away, tossed the Starr on the other side of the room. He hurled Hop Chee away from Jilly, grabbed her neck and hoisted her from the water. Hop spun away as the deputy kept swinging his pistol from Ling to Hop, wondering which one he should cover or shoot.

Jilly's eyes were closed. She appeared not to be breathing. Gunn put his arms around her waist, dragged her from the wooden vat. In so doing, he pushed inward on her diaphragm. Jilly retched.

73

Vomited water. He heard her suck in air, but her throat rattled horribly. He laid her on her belly, straddled her, began to push on the small of her back to expel the water from her lungs.

Hop Chee's right hand slipped behind his back. His eyes glittered as he drew a thin stiletto from its hiding place. Deputy Hall had shifted his gaze to Gunn and Jilly. He watched them with rapt attention, knowing it was a life and death situation. Hop Chee took advantage of the deputy's distraction. Ling was silent, on the floor, gathering her legs beneath her to spring to her husband's aid. Hop Chee padded across the floor, his knife arm rising as he came.

Gunn looked up, just then. Saw Hop Chee.

"Look out!" he warned Hall.

The deputy turned, saw the Chinaman. Hop Chee sprang forward, slashing with the knife. Hall backhanded Hop Chee in the face with the pistol. The knife blade, razor-sharp, grazed his arm. He cried out in pain. Blood gushed up out of the cut, poured through the slit in his sleeve. He chopped downward once again, his pistol hammering Hop Chee's cheekbone. Ling leaped on him from behind, began clawing at the deputy's face. Both Ling and Hop Chee rattled a string of Chinese curses at the deputy.

Gunn pushed hard, forcing water from Jilly's lungs. She coughed and regurgitated. There was very little water. Gunn heard her gasp, turned her over. He bent to her, put his lips against hers and breathed into her mouth. He blew air into her lungs, got them working again. Her eyes fluttered open.

Her black hair was soaked through, her face wet. Gunn got her to her feet. She gasped and spluttered, her eyes wide with fear. She wheezed as her breasts rose and fell, but she was getting air.

"Oh my God!" she exclaimed.

"Take it easy, Jilly. Just get your breath."

Hall had his hands full with Ling. Hop Chee lay stunned on the floor. His hand moved toward the knife, which had fallen from his grasp. Gunn stepped over, kicked it away from him. He reached out, grabbed Ling's long hair, jerked it. She came away from Hall, who appeared bewildered, confused. He wasn't used to fighting with a woman, much less a tigress like the diminutive Ling. Ling turned on Gunn. He didn't waste time with her.

He shot out a hard right. It caught Ling on the tip of her chin, drove her back four feet. Her eyes rolled crazily to the back of their sockets. She crumpled like a broken kite.

Jilly's breathing improved. The wheezing went away. She hadn't swallowed much water. They had broken into the room just in time.

"You all right?" Gunn asked.

"F—f—fine," Jilly said, managing a weak smile.

"Close call."

"Uh huh. Thanks. Both of you. I don't understand. Why?"

Gunn turned to Hop Chee, glared at him.

"Why, Hop Chee?"

Ling burst into tears, crawled to her husband. They put their arms around each other. Hop Chee began crying too.

"Hey, what the hell is this?" Deputy Hall asked.

"Shut up," Gunn said. He looked at the Chinese couple with compassion. They were suffering. They were afraid of something. Someone. "Did Berryman force you to kill Scaggs? Try to kill Miss Collins?" His voice was gentle, his tone soft.

Hop Chee looked up at him with red rimmed eyes. He opened his mouth to speak.

Ling began speaking excitedly in rapid Cantonese. Jilly came up to Gunn, put her arm around his waist. They listened to the woman, not understanding anything except that she was afraid, that she was in anguish.

"Go ahead, Hop Chee, tell us what your wife doesn't want us to know." Gunn gave the deputy a quick glance to shut him up in case he wanted to say something. Hall had his pistol leveled at Hop Chee. "Put your pistol away, Deputy," Gunn said.

Reluctantly, Hall holstered his pistol.

"Ling no want Hop Chee tell you. But I no listen her. You good man. So solly. Tly kill gull and kill man. Bellyman make Hop Chee do this. Ling too. We velly flaid."

"You're afraid? Berryman's not here. He can't hurt you."

"Bellyman take daughter, Soo Li. Him kill gull we don't do what he tell us."

"You say that Berryman kidnapped your daughter? Threatened to kill her if you didn't kill this woman and her mother?"

Hop Chee nodded sadly.

"Oh my god!" Jilly exclaimed.

"Sonofabitch," said Hall. "He does have a daughter. Haven't seen her in a day or so, come to think of it."

"How old is your daughter, Hop Chee?"

"She eighteen."

Jilly gasped.

"Gunn, if she's with . . ."

"Never mind, Jilly. Hop Chee, we'll get your daughter back. But you and your wife are in deep trouble. I don't know if the sheriff will prosecute, but he has that right. You did kill a man. He was a bad man, but you had no right to take his life. You also tried to kill Miss Collins here. That was just as bad. Attempted murder."

"I—I won't press charges," Jilly said.

"I got to take them to jail," Hall said stubbornly.

Gunn gave him a withering look.

Ling spoke in Chinese to her husband. He answered her quickly, explaining what Gunn had said.

"Take them to jail, Deputy," Gunn said, "but explain to Deke Naylor why these people did what they did. Look at them. They're terrified. The real culprit is a man named Jason Berryman. He forced these two to go against their natures. He kidnapped their daughter and he'll make good his threat if we don't stop him."

"I'll do it," said Hall. "Come on you two. On your feet."

A cowed Hop Chee got up, helped Ling to her feet. They went with the deputy, docilely. Ling was still weeping. Hop Chee put his arm around her shoulders.

"Do you feel well enough to leave today?" Gunn asked Jilly.

"Yes. This place gives me the shudders." She

looked at the tub and shivered.

"You want to change? You're all wet."

"I can dry off. Let's go. Quick. When I think of Jason and that young girl . . . There's no telling what he will do to her. I never realized how horrible a man he was. You've got to help me stop him, Gunn. Not for the money, but for the sake of Soo Li."

"I'll stop him. If it's not too late. Speaking of money, I got some of it back for you."

"What? I don't understand."

Grinning, Gunn reached into his pocket. He withdrew a wad of bills and some change. He counted it out in Jilly's hand.

"Four hundred eighty-two dollars and fifty cents," he said.

"That's what Scaggs had left of the five hundred Berryman paid him to kill you and your grandmother."

"Well, I'll be," said Jilly. "Now he only owes me thirty-nine thousand five hundred, more or less."

"He owes you a lot more than that, Jilly," Gunn said grimly. "And he'll pay. He'll pay dearly."

Jilly shivered again. For a different reason.

CHAPTER EIGHT

The young gunny sat on the porch, his chair tilted back against the cabin wall. He held a chunk of soft pine in his hands, whittled it with his knife. He was no more than twenty-two, twenty-three, but there was something old in his pale blue eyes. Old and dead, as if he had seen too much in a short span of time. He was lean, handsome in a vacuous way. One of his shoulders had been broken when he was a dozen years old and had not set right. One shoulder was higher than the other. His left shoulder. It was a distinct advantage as a gunfighter, which he fancied himself to be, because he drew deliberate attention to that shoulder and drew quick with his right arm, the dropped lower shoulder giving him a definite advantage.

Bud Gentry was a hollow man, burned out from something in his guts that had started when he'd killed his first man at fifteen, his uncle Wally. He had a flash temper, a rage that had no origin unless it was something that had come from being beaten by his father and his uncle all his life. Until he had stood up to Wally and blown a hole in his face at pointblank range. That had been in Abilene. He had killed his next man and the one after that, in Tascosa. He didn't like a man, he shot him. That kept people away from him, made men cross the street to avoid him. The law had gotten on him though, and he'd drifted north, up through Colorado, Wyoming, into Montana. Away from people. He stayed too long in a place, men got curious about him. If they bothered him, he shot them until his pistol butt got so notched it had split and he'd had to throw the pieces away. Now he no longer notched his pistol butt, but got himself a grizzly tooth necklace. One tooth for every man he had killed. A dozen now and he still hated, still raged.

In all these years, Bud had never had a man to call friend. Until he had met Jason Berryman. Jason had every bit the outcast he was, but slicker. He knew how to use people. Bud did not. Jason was older, knew a lot. And the same rage he felt burned in Jason. He recognized it in the man's cold dark eyes. Jason didn't fight it. He let it work for him. That's what Bud liked about the man. Berryman didn't get mad, he just got even. Any way he could.

Bud had light hair, a smooth face with no particular distinguishing characteristics. He was only five foot nine, but his boots made him feel taller. He whittled to calm his jangling nerves. He didn't drink, didn't play cards. Like Jason did. Jason was teaching him, though. Paying him for the job he was doing now. An easy job. Watching over the Chinese girl while he made his move at the Mission with the Rawlings woman. Jason could teach him a lot. After they finished up here, they were going on to San Francisco for even bigger pickings. That's what Berryman had promised.

Bud stopped whittling to pick up an Arkansas whetstone. He spit on it, rubbed the blade of the folding Barlow knife against the soft stone. He flipped the blade expertly, holding it at an angle, drawing it across the sharpening stone as he applied pressure. He looked down at the trail, the Mission off in the distance. They were up high here. A fair place to lie low, away from curious people. Jason had found the place, rented it from the widow of an old prospector who had moved to town after her husband had died penniless.

He'd met Jason back in Virginia City, by accident. Sometimes he thought maybe it wasn't an accident, but it might have been. Bud made his living by robbing drunks. It was a way to pick up money without much work and the drunks found it difficult to identify him later. That was one reason why Bud didn't drink. He saw what liquor did to men and they became easy prey for him as he waited in the shadows for the die-hards to leave the saloons.

One night, as he waited in the shadowed passageway between a dry goods store and a cafe, across the street from the Gold Nugget Saloon, a man startled him by walking up on his side of the street almost unnoticed. The man stopped there, lit a cigar and spoke to him.

"If you're waiting for drunks to come out of that saloon, beware. They'll act like drunks, but they'll be detectives."

Bud almost drew his pistol then and shot the man. But something told him the man was trying to help him. He drew away from his spot, circled the dry goods store and waited across the street, next to the Gold Nugget. When the place began closing up, four men staggered out. Each one went to a different passageway across the street. They looked drunk. Feeling he had been hoodwinked, he started to go after one of them. He was low on cash. Just as he was about to step out of the shadows, one of the men straightened up, called to the others.

"Nobody here."

Then, the three other men, sober as judges, joined the first man.

Bud cursed under his breath.

Then the man who had warned him came striding up from a place down the street where he, too, had been hiding.

"See?" he said. "It was a good thing I happened along. I had been drinking with some men in the Nugget and overheard this plan. You know you've about run out your string in this town, feller. I'm Jason Berryman. Come on up to my hotel and we'll smoke a cigar."

Bud admired the man's coolness. And he owed Berryman his life. If he hadn't come along and told him in time, he would have been caught in a deadly crossfire. He still shook when he thought about it.

He finished sharpening his pocket knife and went back to whittling. A few minutes later he saw the lone rider coming up the trail. He grinned, put away his knife and stood up. Jason might have some good news and from the looks of the bundle on the back of his horse, he was bringing needed supplies.

"Howdy, Jason," he said, when the rider came within earshot.

"Hello, Bud. A fine morning." Jason Berryman was tall, thin, moustachioed, sideburned. He had piercing dark brown eyes, black hair. His hair and moustache were thickly pomaded. He always looked, Bud thought, as if he'd just stepped out of a band box. He wore fancy clothes, but was good with a knife or gun. He was a card sharp and a con man. And he could smell money a mile away. Bud though, he was the smartest man he'd ever known.

"You hear any news from Dixon?"

Bud reached up for the sack of stores that Jason untied and handed to him. Jason rode a fine black horse, sat atop a hand-tooled saddle that must have cost a hundred dollars or more. First class, Jason was. Top notch.

Jason swung down from his horse, tied him to the hitchrail. He carefully brushed his clothing, smoothing out the wrinkles. He drew a cheroot from his inside pocket, stuck it in his mouth as he walked up onto the porch, into the shade.

"News, ah yes, Bud. None of it good. The Rawlings Stage came in a while ago. Disaster. Not at all good news, my fine young friend. But we won't worry about it."

That was another thing about Berryman. He was cool of head. Nothing ruffled his feathers.

"But . . . Pete, and that Chinee . . . they . . ."

"They fucked up, Bud, is what they did. Scaggs is dead, the Chink locked up in the hoosegow. The stage driver, Andy MacAndrews, left just after they took the Chink and his old lady to jail. The stupid assholes. Botched the job. Pete nicked the old lady, but there's another fellow in the picture. Name might ring a bell with you."

"Who's that?"

"Gunn."

"The same one that . . ."

"Yeah. Andy's seen him before. He and Jilly are heading this way. Right behind the stage."

Bud whistled.

"Bad medicine. I don't like it. From all I hear about this Gunn, he's wors'n a nest of sidewinders."

"Yeah, I heard the same thing. They talk about him in Virginia City like he's some kind of hero. If he's hooked up with Jilly, there could be trouble."

"How you doin' with the Rawlings woman?"

Jason puffed up with pride.

"Coming along, Bud, coming along. I've got that woman in the palm of my hand. It's only a matter of time."

"From the way you're talking, it don't look like we got much time."

"No. You may be right. How's the girl? You get any of that yet?"

Bud wrinkled his nose in disgust.

"Me and a Chinee gal? You gotta be joshin'. I ain't laid a hand on her. She don't like me much, anyways."

"Nor me, either, I would imagine. Let's take a

84

look. Bring those goods in with you. We'll sit down and run the cards for a while, talk it out. I can't leave the Mission yet. I don't want to blow this deal with Amy Rawlings. It could be worth a lot of money. For both of us.''

Bud grinned. He was quite sure that if he stuck with Jason he'd be a rich man.

Soo Li lay on the bed, her hands tied to the brass posts with strips of linen. Her black hair fell over her forehead in neatly trimmed bangs, shoulder length on the back of her head. She looked up at the two men with bright button eyes, white-rimmed with fear. She was petite, with small breasts, graceful curves under the satiny tunic and pants she wore. Her feet were bare. Her wrists were raw where the linen had chafed them. There was hatred in her eyes, too, but it was smothered by the fear.

''Hungry?'' Jason asked her.

She shook her head.

''Doesn't she eat much?''

Bud shook his head.

''Not much. You get rice? That's what she wants, more'n anything.''

''Yeah. You can cook her up some tonight.''

''Hell, I'll let her do it. She's been doin' the supper anyways.''

''You keep an eye on her, hear?''

''Whatcha gonna do with her now? Ain't no reason to keep her no more.''

Jason lit his cigar, blew out a spume of smoke. He tweaked one side of his moustache.

"Oh, she might come in handy at that. If Gunn knows we have her, which I'm sure he does, she'll do just fine as a hostage with him. Kind of an ace in the hole, you might say."

"Yeah," Bud marveled. That Jason was sure some smart.

Bud unpacked the groceries: rice, beans, eggs, bacon, flour, tea, canned goods, onions, tinned beef, ketchup, tinned ham. He sat at the table, cracked open a new deck of cards.

"You seein' the Rawlings woman tonight, Jason?"

"Yep. Going to pop the question."

"Then what?"

"Oh, I'll tell her I'm having funds transferred from the East. To tide me over, I'll need a few thousand to close a land deal. We can be on our way in a day or so. She has the money. I just have to turn on the charm."

"You sure work slick."

"I try to, Bud. Now, pull up a chair and I'll show you the finer points of dealing." Jason dug into his vest pocket, pulled out a cheap ring with a smooth flat shiny surface. He handed it to Bud. "You wear this ring, turn it under. Then you got yourself a mirror. You practice and soon you'll be able to see the number and suit of every card you deal. Be careful, though. Some men are on to that dodge."

Bud admired the ring, put it on. He turned it over and Jason showed him how to deal so that he could see the cards reflected in his palm. Then he showed him how to deal seconds.

"When you're waiting to score big, the cards will

support you. You won't have to roll drunks."

"Yeah, Jason, I get it. Hell, I'll be a gentleman, just like you."

Jasón disguised his disgust. He needed Bud Gentry. He'd use him until he was no longer useful, then leave him to his fate. With Gunn coming to town, Bud might prove very useful indeed.

Amy Rawlings lived in a nice home in the settlement. It was a two-story frame house. Her father's. After he had died, she inherited his freight business. She had made it go even though the N.P. had threatened to cut into business. She used the railroad to her own advantage, having goods shipped directly to her in Spokane or Missoula and then servicing the isolated towns better than the railroad could. She offered service and speed. The last run had produced a bonus. Andy had found a perfectly good saddle lying alongside the road outside of Hell Gate Canyon. She would sell it and split with him. Money was money.

She combed her short blond hair, wondered how a distinguished gentleman like Jason Berryman could tolerate her freckles. She was not a young woman, nearing thirty, but she was tall, and the freckles came from the skin, skin that was alabaster, almost translucent. She was of Scandinavian stock, born Amy Jurgenson. She and her father were from Minnesota. Her mother died in childbirth. She had married Ed Rawlings, who took over the freight business after her father died and then, on a business trip to southern Oregon Territory, was scalped by the Nez Perce. She had considered moving to one of the big cities, but preferred the open spaces. Besides, she could run the business better from the settlement. Most of her business came from settlers up the Penn Oreille, over at Thompson Falls, Salesh House, Flathead Lake, Fort Owen, Pierce City and Oro Fino. It wasn't a big line, but it had enabled her to buy a restaurant, a theatre and a small saloon, all near the settlement in which she hoped would some day be a big city. Already, quite a few new settlers had come in and she liked them. Mostly, she liked Jason Berryman, who had presented himself as a wealthy investor acting for private interests in Chicago and St. Louis. He was just the kind of man she was looking for. It was time the settlement had some big city sophistication. She was tired of the brawling drunken mix of people who drifted in and out of the town on their way to California and Oregon. Jason Berryman had vision. And he had money.

Tonight would be very special. She sensed it. Jason had said he had a very important question to ask her. Her stomach had leaped a foot when he said that. She had not made love to him, but she knew he wanted her. There had been times when she wished he would ask, but he never had. He was too much a gentleman to presume that she was that kind of woman. But she was that kind of woman. That is, she was lonely, young, eager for romance. Ed had been dead for five years. She'd had no opportunity to bed a man in all that time. Most of the ones she met were too rough, too crude. And, too, the business had taken up a lot of her time. She regretted that.

She made up her mind that if Jason asked the right question, she would invite him to move in with her. People would talk some, but that was all right. She wanted Jason. Wanted him so bad she trembled every time she thought about it.

When the knock on the door came, she was ready. She raced downstairs and opened the door.

Jason Berryman stood there, beaming. He had a box of chocolates under his arm. He looked very dashing. She looked past him and there was a rented buckboard.

"Good evening, Amy. May I come in?"

Her heart soared.

CHAPTER NINE

Gunn and Jilly followed the St. Regis, up through Sohan Pass.

The late start had put them there at dusk. Gunn decided to make camp in one of the canyons in the Bitterroots. They would be out of the way, have privacy. He threaded his way through stunted pines willows and cottonwoods, the short grass sear, dry in the late summer. He found a sheltered flat spot near a trickling spring, a place for the horses to graze hobbled.

Shadows deepened in the canyon as the sun fell away. Gunn gathered dry twigs, deadwood, while Jilly set their bedrolls out. The fire was for warmth companionship. They chewed on dry biscuits, jerky opened a can of tomatoes. The temperature dropped off sharply as the last glow of daylight faded in the sky. Above them, they heard the *whucker whucker whucker* of a sharp-tailed grouse, disturbed from its evening bed.

"Likely Berryman'll be expecting us," Gunn said, rolling a cigarette as he sprawled by the fire. Jilly sat next to him, her legs drawn up, staring into the dancing flames.

"In Cataldo Mission?"

"If he's there. Freight wagon pulled out like a bat out of hell before we left. Should be pulling into the town about now."

"I didn't notice."

"Saw the driver talking to Deputy Hall. Then he lit a shuck."

"How far is it to the Mission from here?"

"About thirty miles."

"What if Jason's not there?"

"We go on."

Jilly smiled at him.

"You're awful nice to be with me on this, Gunn. I feel good about it, for the first time. You know, when my grandmother and I were following him from St. Louis, he stayed a few days in almost every town, longer in the larger ones. I think he'll still be there. Working one of his schemes."

"It's likely. It's a long piece down the Mullah Road, crossing the snake to Walla Walla. Figure he'll eventually want to pick up the Oregon Trail unless he doubles back on us. Man like that, though, will probably keep going west to new country. Maybe change his name. There's a pattern there."

"Except Jason won't change his name. He's very arrogant. Very proud."

"Pride brings a man down."

Jilly looked at Gunn, as if trying to assess his

dimensions in a different environment. He seemed perfectly at home here, attuned to a world she only dimly remembered. For a moment, she lost all sense of time, imagined that she was sitting there with her father. He had taught her to hunt, to fish, to enjoy the outdoors, but she had never had many quiet hours with him. Like this, with Gunn. There had been some times when they had just sat and talked, or didn't talk, and she had missed those times. Now, it was as if they were being given back to her, with this man, this strange, silent man who was strong, who had given her so much in so short a time.

"Gunn?"

"Huh?"

"What did—did your wife call you?"

"Billy."

"You don't like the name anymore." It was a flat statement.

"It's not my name anymore. Billy died when Laurie died. I wasn't the same man anymore."

"I don't understand. I want to, but I don't."

He sighed, blew a plume of smoke up into the air. Watched it disintegrate in the vagrant breeze that stirred the grasses, worried the fire.

"I had something to do. Billy couldn't do it. I had to find Laura's killers, make them pay. I became a different man, with a different name. Gunnison was a young hothead who fought in the War. Billy was Laurie's husband, her lover. Gunn was somebody new. Somebody who could get a hard job done. One who could kill a man for good reason."

"And did you kill the man who murdered your wife?"

92

"No. A man didn't murder her."

"Oh?"

"A woman killed her, Jilly. Her best friend."

Jilly sucked in her breath. She was shocked. Shocked at what Gunn had told her, shocked at herself for going so deeply into this man's mind. His face was the same. Handsome, rough, the pale gray eyes that said nothing, yet said everything. The face that concealed what was inside him. The good and the bad.

"Gunn. I'm sorry."

"Don't be. That was a long time ago."

"I mean I'm sorry I asked. It wasn't proper of me."

He tossed his quirly into the fire, reached out, touched her hand.

"Who are you, Jilly? Now."

"I—I don't really know. Somehow, at this moment, Jason Berryman doesn't seem important. The money certainly isn't. Revenge is such a terrible thing, isn't it? You know, don't you?"

"I know. It is a terrible thing. It twists the man who has it more than it does the man he's out to make pay. But it's human, too. I guess I'm as human as anybody else."

"Yes, Gunn. You are."

She rolled over to him, nestled in his arms. She felt safe there. He held her tightly as they both stared into the fire, thinking. It was a long time before either of them spoke. Finally, Jilly looked up at him, turning in his arms like a burrowing creature.

"I want you, Gunn. I haven't been able to think

about anything else all day. Even—even when I thought I was drowning, I thought about you, me, what we did together.''

"Come on, Jilly," he said. "Let's go to bed." He kicked on the fire as Jilly undressed, crawled into the bedroll. Gunn joined her when the fire was out, slipped in beside her, naked. Jilly pulled the blankets over them, snuggled into his arms. They kissed.

"It's warm," she said. "You're warm."

Her body was soft, pliant. She nestled against him and moved her hand to his loins. Grasping his stalk, she stretched up, kissed his mouth. Squeezed him hard. The stalk grew in her hand, throbbed. He touched a breast, smoothed it with his hand. His finger toyed with the nipple. The rubbery nubbin stiffened, flared with rushing blood. She wriggled in his arms.

He entered her slow. She looked up at his face against a backdrop of stars sprinkled on blue velvet sky. Her hand played with his hair as he stroked in and out of her, plumbing the dank heat of her sex with slow sure movements. He rose and fell above her like a slow surging tide as her body responded in matching rhythms interrupted by sudden climactic spasms. He sank into her warm wet depths, burying his shaft in the pulsating folds of her sex, exulting in the electric shivers that sang through his flesh.

She curled her legs around his back, rocking with him. He stroked her breasts, fondling them as he looked down at her moonlit face, the dark hollows of her eyes. Her hands held onto his wide back, gently kneading the muscles as sporadic explosions

94

jolted her senses, lifted her to dizzying heights of ecstasy. She cooed and purred like some small contented animal.

"Oh, Gunn, it's so beautiful this time."

The scent of pines drifted to their nostrils. The dripping spring played a gentle tune as it rippled over the rocks, dripping in a pool. The horses snorted, grazing quietly, hobbled to keep them near. The night sky winked in a dazzling display light years away, interminable, rhythmic, timeless. A lone owl floated over them silently hunting, almost invisible. A wolf howled on a distant peak, the echoes of its cry dying in the deep dark canyons, swallowed by the earth and the night itself.

He let her have her head, taking her to even higher peaks than before. He drove her on until she was screaming and clawing, until he raced with her, pounding into her faster and faster until their movements blurred into one crashing climax that sucked the air out of their lungs, drained their muscles of power and shattered their thoughts into shards as reality was blotted out in one volcanic moment.

Sweat drenched their naked bodies. Jilly kicked off the blankets and lay there, her legs spread wide, letting the breeze blow her dry and cool. Gunn lay beside her, his lungs heaving, a feeling of intense satisfaction flowing through his veins. A shooting star blazed silver across the sky as if some god had struck a match in the vault of the heavens. The star winked off somewhere out in space. An owl hooted somewhere off to their left, a lone wide-eyed sentinal silhouetted in a scrub pine.

Later, they slept, the blankets drawn over them in their nakedness.

They slept until almost noon.

"There's no hurry," Gunn assured her. "I want to get there after dark anyway. Berryman may be looking for you. Or have a spotter."

"You have an idea?"

"Yes. I don't want him to know you're in town for a while. So, you're going to register under a different name. I'll see if I can get a bead on him, or draw his fire."

"Not literally, I hope."

"No. A figure of speech, you might say."

They came into the settlement after dark, drifting off the main road, following the scattered lights of cabins, houses, to come to the main street by a little-used route. Gunn left Jilly in a safe place while he reconnoitered. He rode up the main street from the west, picked out the biggest hotel in town, The Coeur d'Alene Hostelry, and hitched his horse to the rail, went inside. The lobby was empty, the clerk disinterested. He registered under the single name, Gunn. Paid the fee. He went up to his room, dropped off his saddle bags, rifle, bedroll and canteen. He stalled for a while, went back down through the lobby. The clerk didn't give him a second look.

"You register there," he told Jilly. "I'm in room fourteen. I'll scout around town for a couple of hours. Slip a note under my door telling me what room you're in. You're Miss Smith from San Francisco. Don't let the hotel clerk get a good look at your face. I don't want you to leave your room. I'll have your meals sent in. Hungry now?"

"No. But I'll miss you, Gunn."

"I'll come to you. You stay put. In your room. Clear?"

"I guess so."

"Fine. I'll board your horse. Don't chit chat with the clerk. If he asks any questions, ignore him. He doesn't look too curious, but he may be in Jason's pay."

"You're suspicious of everyone."

He grinned.

A block from the hotel, he watched her dismount. He rode on, leading her horse to the livery stables. The street was quiet. Lucky. The settlement looked fairly new. The Mission itself was north of the settlement. Every so often he saw lights blinking in the hills; between the buildings, the lamplit windows of houses.

He passed two or three saloons. The most promising was Stillman's. He heard music, loud talk, women's laughter. He found Canby's Livery, *horses boarded, shod, day, week, month*. It was closed, but the door was open. There was a sign on the door. *Hours 7:00 to 7:00. Leave horses overnight in empty stalls. $1.00 a night, 50¢ for hay and grain. Payable in morning*. He led the horses inside, found stalls for them, hung the saddles and bridles up on the nails driven into the outside posts. He dumped hay in their bins. They didn't need grain yet. Tomorrow would do.

It was a two block walk to the hotel, a block to Stillman's. Gunn passed false fronts proclaiming *Loan Agent, Meat Market, Bar, Advocate Office, Drug Store, Dress Shop, Post Office, Sheriff, Bar, Fruits & Cold Drinks, Dry Goods* and *Clothing, Beer Hall, Amy's Home Restaurant, Rawlings Freight Line* (Brokers & Shippers), *Stoves & Hardware, Groceries*, all jammed close together, clapboarded in haste. There was a store that said *Signs* out front and there were several signs stacked in the window. There was no boardwalk, lots of hitchrails.

Stillman's Saloon advertised nickel beer, music, dancing, whiskey. A sign over the batwing doors said: *Pride of the West* in flowing script. There were wooden carvings of girls, painted over in bright colors that flanked the doors, signed by someone named Arnold. The girls wore can-can outfits and showed thighs and garterbelts as they kicked up their heels and smiled at incoming patrons or passersby.

Gunn went inside, his eyes adjusting quickly to the bright lights. Lanterns hung at intervals from high beams, on podiums along the walls and on the mirrored backbar. There was a small dance floor, roped off, a honky tonk piano and a small bandstand. Pretty fancy for a one-horse town. The place had two stories, an area for card playing and tables for drinking and eating. Sawdust, both coarse and fine, littered the tobacco juiced floor. There were butts of cigars and cigarettes mingled in with the sawdust; a few spittoons attested to the inaccuracy of the chewers. They were clean, unsullied.

Gunn walked to the bar, found a spot at the end

where he could look over the assemblage. Several pairs of eyes followed him to the bar, looked away after he put his foot up on the rail. He ordered a whiskey from a burly bartender with the puffed eyes of a fighter, either a pugilist or a brawling lumberjack, Gunn figured. He paid the man four bits, looked around as he took a swig.

Then he saw her, across the room.

She was tall, almost statuesque. She had short blond hair, freckles, an hourglass figure. She was dressed becomingly in an evening dress that hugged her curvaceous figure. Her milkmaid breasts bulged underneath her bodice. Her skin was as pale as milk.

Their eyes met for an instant.

She stood next to a man at a table, playing cards. The man's back was turned to Gunn. He wore a low-crowned black hat, was lean, narrow in the shoulders.

Gunn smiled at the woman.

She started to smile back, looked at his dusty clothes, thought better of it.

Gunn touched a finger to the brim of his hat, lifted his glass to her.

The man at the table turned around then, looked at Gunn.

Gunn recognized him from Jilly's description. The thin moustache, the lean cruel face.

Jason Berryman.

Gunn finished his whiskey, left the bar.

Later, he would make his move.

CHAPTER TEN

"Who was that?" Jason asked Amy. There was a trace of annoyance in his voice. He was losing and Jason didn't like to lose.

"I haven't any idea," she said. "Stranger."

"Well, he acted a little too bold, if you ask me."

"Yes," she mused. "He did, didn't he?"

Jason saw the look in Amy's eyes. Something twitched in his brain. His face blanched slightly. He turned back to the cards, threw in his hand.

"I've had enough. Thanks, boys. I'll get you next time."

"Better luck tomorrow night, Mr. Berryman," said one of the men. "Ain't often we get to keep your money overnight."

Hearty laughter at the table. Berryman stood up.

"Let's go home," he said. "I shouldn't have sat in that game anyway."

"But, Jason, you know I had some business to

take care of. It was perfectly all right. It's just a game.''

It wasn't the game he was thinking about now. Amy was not a tease. She liked people, but she was no flirt. Yet she had been attracted to that man at the bar. Who was he? He had never seen him before, but there was something about him that was familiar. If it was Gunn, then that meant Jilly was probably in town. But if it was Gunn, why hadn't he said anything? Made his move? It was unnerving.

He and Amy had dined at her restaurant. Afterwards, he'd ordered champagne. Then, when he was about to give her the ring, one of her employees had come in and said she was needed at Stillman's the saloon she owned. While she had taken care of business, he had played cards. He was distracted at being interrupted before he could make his proposal, and he lost his concentration. And several hands of cards.

"What was it that was so important here, anyway?" he asked. "Couldn't it have waited?"

Amy recoiled for an instant at his sharp tone.

"Yes, it was important. One of my boys got hurt. I had to make arrangements for someone to take his place on tomorrow's stage to Spokane. I run a business, Jason. You know that."

He took her arm, led her to the back hallway. The buggy was hitched out back. The one he'd rented as part of his bid for Amy's hand.

"I'm sorry, Amy. It's just that I was counting on being alone with you tonight. I—I have something important to talk to you about and . . ."

"I understand," she soothed. "We'll go to my

place and pick up where we left off. In fact, I had Pat put two bottles of chilled champagne in your buggy.''

"That was very thoughtful of you, my dear." He cursed himself. He had almost jeopardized his romance with Amy Rawlings. He didn't want her to see any display of temper, although he had one. Nothing must come between him and his goal. Amy was a fish, almost hooked, and he couldn't afford to stir up the waters at this stage of the scheme. He hoped he had been properly apologetic with her.

They walked out the back. He helped her into the buggy, untied the reins. As he climbed in, he peered around in the dark. Wondering.

"Anything wrong?" she asked.

"No. It's just that I always keep an eye out for footpads in places like this."

"Jason, we haven't had that kind here since the mines petered out. Don't worry."

The horse clopped down the alley, turned the corner, went down the main street.

Behind them, in the livery, Gunn watched them pass by. Buck was saddled again. When the buggy was far enough away, he led the horse out, mounted up. He rode, keeping his distance, keeping to the shadows.

At Amy's house, Jason helped her down from the buggy. He carried the champagne. He had the odd feeling that they had been followed, but he didn't want to make a point of it. Amy could never know about Jilly—and Gunn. But once on her porch he peered off in the distance, trying to see if anyone was out there. He saw no one. But the feeling persisted. He wasn't sure that the man he had seen at Stillman's was Gunn, but he could have been. The timing would be about right. Yet the man had said nothing, had given no sign. Maybe he was getting spooked. Those women had frazzled his nerves. He couldn't wait until they were out of the way.

Gunn had stopped when the buggy pulled up to the house. He still didn't know who the woman was, but he would find out in time. He was sure that this was her home, not Jason's. He tied his horse to a bush, walked to the house on foot, coming at it from the side, staying to the shadows. He would never find out where Soo Li was if he had to kill Jason now. And he might not even be able to recover Jilly's money for her. But in the meantime, he had to find out everything he could about Jason, his habits, where he lived, who were his friends. He hoped that the woman had no dogs. As if reading his thoughts, a dog barked. A block away. Gunn froze, then went on, as lamps were lit in the big house.

Amy poured two glasses of champagne. Her living room was large, comfortable, feminine. Overstuffed divan and chairs, fine tables from St. Louis, lamps from Chicago and Denver, fancy doilies, a rolltop desk, a fireplace, mantle, Currier & Ives prints in gilded frames on the walls. Jason had been there before, but now he took a renewed interest in the house. He might be staying here instead of at the Coeur d'Alene. At least long enough for Amy to put more money into his coffers.

Taking money from women was a deadly serious game with Jason. He hated women. Their sexual power. In truth, although he did not know this, he was afraid of women. In fearing them, he hated them. As a child, his mother had fussed over him, sissified him, praised him. As he grew older, however, he realized that his mother was jealous of other women, girlfriends. She did her best to break up every relationship with a female that he developed. As a result, he began to subconsciously fear his mother and all women. Then, when his romances failed, that fear turned to hate.

He would not have rationalized his attitude in this way, but he knew part of it. Women were too strong. Men killed for them. Men were humiliated by them. Jason took their money. He stole part of their power. He humiliated them. It was revenge against his mother whom he had grown to hate in later years. Whom he hated now. His mother, after he had left home for good, had taken to using opium, which was plentiful in the East. She had been a wealthy, attractive woman. Now, she was a hopeless addict, living only for the dreams that opium could give her.

"Now," Amy said, with a sigh. "What shall we drink to, Jason?"

He stood up. "To you, Amy."

"Why thank you, Jason," she said, disappointed. "I was hoping that . . . oh, never mind."

"Amy, I won't apologize again for being upset that our evening had to be interrupted. But, when I tell you why, you may understand."

Her eyelashes fluttered coyly. She sat primly on

the divan. Jason sat in a chair, facing her.

He reached into his pocket, pulled out a sma[ ]
package.

Handed it to her.

"Why, Jason, whatever have you gone an[ ]
done?"

"Open it," he said. He had gone through this s[ ]
many times, he could do it blindfolded. He kne[w]
what she would say, and what he would say. [I]
worked every time. Like a charm.

She opened the wrapping carefully, trying not t[ ]
appear too eager.

A small box. A ring inside. A diamond engage[ ]
ment ring.

"Oh, Jason, you shouldn't have . . . oh, my, it'[ ]
so—so beautiful. Simply exquisite." She held it u[p]
to the light, turning it over in her fingers. The ligh[t]
caught the diamond, shot through its prisms[ ]
glistened like a bursting star.

He rose from his seat, went to her.

"Here, Amy, let me put it on you." He slippe[d]
the ring on her middle finger, left hand.

"Jason? Does this mean . . . oh, I didn't dar[e]
think . . ."

He smiled benignly.

"Amy, I've come to ask your hand in marriage[.]
That is, if you think . . ."

She grasped his head with both hands, kissed hi[m]
smackingly on the lips.

"Oh, you sweet man you! Of course I'll marr[y]
you! Jason, you've made me the happiest woman o[n]
earth!"

"Can we set the date?"

"Oh, yes. Whenever you say."

"No, you. As soon as possible."

Amy was flustered. "Oh, my. Oh, me. I just don't know what to say. This is all so sudden. I mean, I have to buy a trousseau, make arrangements . . ."

He took her in his arms, kissed her impetuously on the lips. He could feel her pounding heart beneath her breast.

"Amy, do we need all that? I mean, does it have to be all that fancy? Couldn't we just, well, get married quietly. By a judge or minister? It's not as if we have to publish the Banns."

"I don't know, Jason. This is a big step. A big event for the settlement. I have friends. Don't you want to invite some of your Chicago friends out? Your family?"

"No. I—I'm an orphan, Amy. My family all died in a fire when I was a baby."

"Oh, you poor man. I'm sorry. Of course. We'll get married right away. It's silly of me, a woman of my age. Oh, Jason, you've made me so happy!"

Gunn stood by the window, eavesdropping. He could hear the pair very clearly. He stood so that he could not be seen, but could see Amy and Jason. He knew her first name, not her last. He wondered if she was the owner of the restaurant that bore her name, and he gathered that she must have some interest in Stillman's too.

As Gunn watched, Jason took Amy in his arms, kissed her earlobes, her neck, until the woman was squirming with desire.

"You've made me very happy, Amy," Jason said.

"I wish we were married now. I hate to leave."

"Must you, Jason? After all, we're not children. I have a big house here."

"It might not be seemly."

"Do you want to stay, Jason?"

"Far be it for me to go against such a beautiful woman's wishes, my dear. If you will have the gentleman to your quarters, I would be most grateful to accept." His mock graciousness brought a smile to Amy's lips. She curtsied politely in acknowledgment of his high-flown talk.

"Oh, Jason, you're so much fun!"

"Let me put the horse and buggy up for the night. I'll join you shortly."

Gunn froze.

He looked around for a place to hide. The only place suitable was next to the porch, and only if he hugged the ground, lay perfectly still. He backed away from the window, crawled on his hands and knees to the side of the porch. He lay flat just as the front door slammed. Jason's boots clumped across the hardwoods, then grew muffled in the dust.

Jason put the horse up in the stables out back, then returned, while Gunn still held his frozen position by the porch. He was about to rise when the front door slammed. Amy met Jason on the porch. He heard them talking, sipping champagne.

"It's such a beautiful evening, I thought we'd finish our cocktails out here," said Amy.

Gunn cursed silently.

The two sat in the porch swing. The swing creaked as they swayed to and fro, bundling, making small love talk. Gunn's knee was jammed onto a rock. He didn't dare move. The rock dug into his flesh. In his mind, the rock grew in size and sharpness. He heard the sounds of the two lovers kissing, the gurgle of champagne down their throats. They were right over him, not six feet away. He controlled his breath, afraid of discovery.

"More champagne, Jason?"

"No thanks. I think we ought to retire."

"My, you're so formal this evening."

"I feel formal. I just proposed to a most wonderful woman. And she has accepted. Not only that, she is willing to consummate the marriage a few days early."

"Oh, yes, Jason. I do."

Gunn heard them kiss again. The swing creaked as their weight was released from it. Footsteps clattered across the porch. The front door slammed. He let out a sigh, lifted his leg off the offending stone. He picked it up, surprised at how small it was. A pebble really. He dusted himself off, walked to the window again. Nearby, a dog barked. A moment later it howled with pain.

Jason blew out the lamps, all but one, then followed Amy upstairs.

Gunn had seen enough.

He started to walk away from the window, when he heard a sound.

Out of the corner of his eye, a shadow loomed. As he was about to turn around, he saw something flash. Something hard, steely, crashed into his skull. Lights blossomed in his brain. He twisted, reflexively, and a shapeless face danced before his eyes. Then, a swallowing darkness rose up and enveloped him. He felt himself falling from a great height. Falling until he crashed into a black pool. The dark waters washed over his mind, blotting out all pain, all sensation.

Bud Gentry stood over the fallen Gunn, a smirk on his lips.

He holstered his pistol after checking to see if he'd broken the grips.

"I don't know who you are mister," he said, "but you ain't got no business spying on Jason."

He knew his words went unheard.

He lifted Gunn by the shoulders, dragged him around to the front of the house.

It was a good thing he'd seen the man sneaking around Amy Rawlings' house before he'd ridden up. The man was big, heavy. He wondered who he was. Jason would wonder too. But Jason, as he saw through the window, was busy. He wouldn't want to be disturbed now. But the clerk had come up to the cabin with an urgent message. A young woman fitting the description of Jill Collins had checked into the hotel earlier. The clerk, Amos Dunbar, had been unable to leave until the night clerk had come on. The woman had registered under the name of Smith, but he was sure that was a phony name. Bud knew that Jason would want to be informed right away, but now he might not want to hear about the girl or this man until tomorrow. Bud was smart enough to know that Jason was going to put the boots to Amy Rawlings and it wouldn't do to spoil that. Too much money involved.

Bud had become suspicious when he saw the horse tied up, unattended. A buckskin. Now he knew why. This man had sneaked up to Amy's house, had been spying on Jason. Well, he'd take him to the cabin and tie him up. Jason would be out early in the morning. He'd be proud that Bud had known what to do.

Gentry stripped Gunn of his knife and pistol, slapped his face. He held Gunn's .45 up to his face as Gunn's eyes fluttered.

"One word, pilgrim, and I blow out your fuckin' lights."

CHAPTER ELEVEN

Amy was a roughhouse lover.

Full of energy, amply proportioned, she was more than a handful for Jason Berryman.

Naked, she resembled the women in those paintings by Rubens. Jason played with her for ten minutes, suckling her breasts, fondling her cunny while she cooed and sighed like a schoolgirl. She handled his swollen rod as if it was a pump handle, jerking it up and down, squeezing it until Jason almost winced with pain. But he kept his feelings to himself. He knew, however, after the first few minutes of their love romp, that he had his hands full with the big corn-fed Minnesota Swede. She bounced on his lean frame with rib-cracking intensity, rollicking with the joy of at last touching a man, exploring his naked body with eager hands, gushing enthusiasm. The memory of farm boys in hay lofts was still strong in her mind, and her husband had been cold and buried for five years.

Jason, for his part, couldn't wait to get the act over with. He hadn't counted on Amy's unfettered ebullience. Rather, he had thought she would be rather shy, reserved. Instead, she had stripped out of her clothes like a two-dollar hurdy-gurdy gal and had leaped on him like a hippo seconds after he'd crawled into her large feather bed. The bed rocked like a freight car down a Rocky Mountain grade, the slats creaking under the twin weights, threatening to crack every time she bounced.

She squealed and shrieked as he prepared to mount her.

"I'm so excited, Jason. I think I came ten times already."

"Good. I'm glad, Amy."

She spread her ample thighs, prepared to receive him. Her body seemed to be perpetually jiggling, as if it were composed of gelatin. Still, she was a handsome woman and he was happy that she was so easily satisfied. He had little patience with frosty women. If they couldn't attain a climax in the short span of time he alloted to the love act, then they were just out of luck. Jason was a rabbit. He lasted until his own gratification was assured, and that was all.

He plummeted down toward her and sank between her legs, his shaft oozing into her like a hot knife through butter. Amy rocked with pleasure, her pneumatic body squirming as he skewered her with his throbbing tool. A high-pitched squeal issued from her throat. She thrashed wildly as orgasmic spasms convulsed her before he had even fully entered her.

"Oh my! she shrieked. "Ohhhhhhhh Jasoooonnnnnnnnn! Holy Moses!

Her energetic gyrations served to block him from his own quest for pleasure. Grimly determined, Jason plowed on, plunging in and out of her furiously, hanging on to her bouncing body for dear life. Amy wallowed like a boat that had lost its keel, flesh jiggling, breasts bobbing up and down, legs kicking and thrashing.

"Fuck me, Jason," she shrieked, "fuck me blind!"

"Amy, Amy, Amy . . . ummmmmmm!

Jason became caught up in Amy's frenzied search for sensation. Despite himself. Her pendulous breasts thwacked into each other as she tossed from side to side, great bulbous melons that seemed to have a life of their own. He dipped down and took a nipple between his teeth, worried it, teethed it, until he thought Amy was going to pound his back to a pulp. The nipple hardened into a rubbery acorn and he left, went on to the other, nibbled it until Amy once again bucked with orgasm. He felt as if she was swallowing him up, devouring him with constantly moving landslides of flesh, avalanches of alabaster skin that slid from breast to thigh and back the other way as she tilted herself by thrusting upward or crashing downward into the soft feather mattress.

"Jason, I love you, darling. I'll marry you and fuck you day and night. Oh, fuck me, keep on fucking me!"

He was glad there was no one in the house. Glad that they weren't in the hotel. Her voice reverberated in the room, bouncing off the walls until the very house vibrated.

He lasted longer than he thought he would, from the sheer hysteria of Amy's gyrations. But his own desire caught up with him and he felt his seed rush from its sac in a headlong burst. He shot into her while she sobbed and hammered on his back with fists until he had to wrench himself free. She didn't want him to pull out of her and she held on, screaming at him to stay, to stay.

"Oh, I can't," he gasped. "I'm spent. Fair spent, Amy."

She released him then, and he tumbled gratefully away from her.

Amy immediately rolled on top of him and embraced him in a suffocating bear hug.

"I love you, sweet Jason. I'm yours, all yours."

And Jason saw his opportunity, although the moment was not exactly right.

An hour later, as they lay talking in sleepy
ones, Jason took advantage of the opportunity.

"Amy."

"Yes, Jason?"

"I have a small problem. I doubt if you can
elp, but I want you to know about it."

She sat up, fully awake, the languor tossed off
ike a nightcap.

"Jason, let me help. I want to help."

"It—it's not a serious problem. Just temporary.
You know I want to marry you right away.
Tomorrow if I could. The next day, certainly. And
want you to be wed in style. Then I will buy you
he prettiest things a woman could want. I'll spoil
ou with riches.

"I don't want anything but you, my darling."

Jason smiled in the dark, building up to his
oint with linguistic precision. His pauses were
regnant with meaning. His intonation was perfect-
y attuned. He had done this many times before.
He had practiced his halting little speeches before a
irror until they were little gems of persuasion,
erfectly constructed masterpieces of Machiavellian
ogic.

"The truth is, I'm a little short of funds. Oh,
's a temporary condition. In my haste to close a
ew deals for my clients out here, I neglected to
over my expenses to the fullest contingency. I'll
end off a wire to Chicago from Missoula soon's I
an get over there. The problem is that would take
he some time, back and forth, and I must close

this deal within two days or lose my option. I—overextended myself, had to dip into my own funds. Not unusual, and sometimes I make pretty good side deals for my own company, but in this case, I'm strapped. If I go to Missoula tomorrow I could be tied up for days there, waiting for letters of credit, bank drafts and authorizations. In the meantime, this deal could slip through my fingers."

He let the impact of his words settle on Amy. He could see that she was both concerned and fascinated. Large dollar figures, enormous land deals, secretive machinations behind the scenes of big business, never failed to impress a gullible woman. Her eyes were wide as buttons, her ponderous breasts rose and fell with the heave of her breathing. She was hooked for fair. He had delivered his oratory with the proper pitch, the exact intonation, the perfect rhythm.

"Jason, this is silly. You don't have to go to all that trouble. I can advance you the funds you need. I can have the stage driver deliver your telegram to the Western Union in Missoula on the next trip. And he can pick up your funds or all those other things when they come in. He's bonded. All of my drivers are bonded."

"It's a considerable amount, I'm afraid. I wouldn't want to put you to any trouble."

"How much?" There was a touch of wariness in her voice.

Jason knew that the amount was crucial. If

was too high, he'd scare her off. If it was too low, he would cheat himself.

"Fifteen thousand would close the deal," he said off-handedly. "I realize it's not much of a sum to bother about, but I'm putting up fifty thousand of my own funds and I'm short that much. The total outlay is sixty-five thousand. I might be able to get the deal delayed twenty-four hours, but there are other bidders . . ."

He let it hang there, let it soak in.

Bullshit. All bullshit. Some people could smell it. A woman who was in love seldom could.

Amy looked at Jason in the half dark. She grabbed his arms, squeezed.

"Don't you worry about this, Jason. I'll have that money to you by noon tomorrow."

"You're a dear, Amy. Of course I'll give you a note and have it back to you in a week, ten days."

"Don't be silly. What's mine is yours, Jason."

That was all he wanted to hear.

Gunn knew what the sound was that he had heard before being coldcocked by the gunny.

A faint rattle. Those grizzly teeth hanging from the man's neck.

He should have paid more attention to the barking dog. To a lot of things.

He marked his bearings well as they rode up into the hills above the Mission. His hands were tied behind his back. Tied tight, with leather thongs cut from his new saddle.

That damned necklace rattled behind him.

Why hadn't the man alerted Jason? Who was he? Was he after Jason, too?

No, that didn't seem likely.

There was some connection between the two.

After they got inside the cabin he knew.

Soo Li stared at him with blinking eyes. She lay there, tied to the bed, the lamp light scratching at her sleep-filled eyes.

Gentry shoved Gunn roughly into the room.

"Gotcha a bedmate, Chinee gal," he said, in his slow Texas drawl.

Soo Li's face showed no emotion. It was an Oriental mask.

"You," he said to Gunn, "down on the floor, buster." He tapped Gunn's shoulder with the barrel of his .45. Gunn sat. Gentry holstered his pistol and he untied Soo Li's hands, moved her over to one side of the bed. Then he retied her, cut new strips for her ankles. He lashed her, hands and feet, to a single post on the far side of the bed. "All right, buster, up on the bed, stretch out."

Bud left the thongs on Gunn's wrists, cut up a manila rope in varying lengths. He tied Gunn up in the same fashion, after removing his boots. Then he lashed the remaining length of rope across the two at the waist. Satisfied, he looked at Gunn with vacuous pale blue eyes.

"I'll be sleepin' in the bunk in the next room. I hear you trying to get loose, I'll lay a gunbarrel acrost your skull, buster."

Gunn said nothing, watched as the man took the

amp into the next room, closed the door. He and Soo Li were left in darkness, securely bound.

Gunn cursed himself for a fool. He had let himself get caught like some dumb yokel. He still wondered how the man could have gotten so close without being heard. The man was like a cat. He hadn't heard a sound until the gunny was right on top of him. No ordinary man could step that quiet in boots.

He listened to the sounds in the next room. The gunny was preparing to go to bed. He was pretty quiet, even so. Habit? Practice? He twisted his head to see the light under the door. There was nothing to do but wait. He had no doubt the man would make good his threat if he tried to get free of his bonds. His head throbbed now, a lump there where he'd been cracked on the skull. Next to him, he heard the Chinese girl breathing evenly. He wondered if she could speak English. Probably. Her father could. He didn't know about her mother. He had never heard Ling speak anything but Chinese and a few garbled words of English.

The lamp went out in the next room.

Gunn waited, wide awake. From the sound of her breathing, he knew Soo Li was awake, too. The minutes crawled by. His ears strained to pick up sound in the next room. It was quiet. Then he heard the man turn over on the cot. Asleep? Perhaps. There was no way of telling, for sure.

Gunn moved his wrists. The thongs bit into the flesh, but the man hadn't wetted them down. They would give, in time. The rope was another matter. It

wasn't new rope. Soft, pliable, it had been draw
tight on his wrists and ankles. The trick was to wor
the bonds right. If he pulled the wrong way, the
would only tighten. The man had used a timb
hitch. If he pulled too hard, the rope also wou
tighten up on him.

He felt an elbow jab him in the ribs.

Startled, he twisted toward the girl. He could n
see her face in the dark, only the dim dark outli
of her bulk on the bed next to him.

"Come close," she whispered.

He stretched his neck as far as he could. He sa
that she was doing the same.

"I am almost free," she said, her voice very lo
and soft.

He made no reply but he could hear the rust
of her wrists working at the knotted linen. The
was no sound from the next room. Finally, he fe
a hand on his chest.

"I'm free," she said. Her accent was sligh
There was none of the difficulty with the L-soun
her father had. "Be quiet. After I untie my feet,
will untie you. We must be careful."

"Yes."

He saw her shape rise up and her hands wor
quickly, deftly, at her ankle bonds.

A few moments later, he breathed a sigh
relief. Soo Li had untied his wrists so that h
could then untie his ankles. He rubbed his wrist
touched the knot on his head.

He turned to face her. She touched his fac
drew him close, whispered in his ear.

"What will you do now?" she asked.

"We have to get out of here." Her touch was delicate. There was something exciting about being so close to her in the dark. "It could be dangerous."

"I know."

"Soo Li. I'm Gunn. Your father and mother are all right."

"Thank you. No more talk."

She was right. His mind raced. If they tried to crawl through the window, they would make too much noise. He would be unarmed, afoot. The man in the next room could easily track them, shoot them down. It was too risky.

He tried to remember where the bunk was located in the next room. His mind went over every detail even though he'd not had much time to look at anything when the man shoved him through it. The bunk was to the right of the door, which opened outward. Three or four strides after he opened the door. Had it creaked when the man had closed it? He didn't think so. Still, the man might be a light sleeper. He almost certainly would have a pistol in his hand or close enough to reach in a split second.

There was only one thing to do. After considering all the possibilities, he whispered to Soo Li.

She nodded. Moments later, she slipped from the bed. They felt their way in the dark. Gathered up blankets stacked on a shelf. Arranged them on the bed by feel. Only a thin streak of moonlight penetrated the room through the boarded windows. Gunn saw then that they could never have gotten out that way. Finally, they were finished.

"Now," he whispered, stationing her in a corner of the room, "when I make the sign, you do what I told you."

He padded quietly to the left side of the door, stood there.

Gunn hoped like hell his plan would work.

CHAPTER TWELVE

Gunn bunched his muscles, went into a crouch. He was ready.

His arm shot out in a signalling gesture.

Soo Li screamed.

She kept screaming, louder and louder. Her screams reverberated in the small room, shattering the silence of the night. It sounded, Gunn thought with a wry grin, as if she were being murdered—or raped.

The door burst open. Bud Gentry leaped inside on stockinged feet, his pistol cocked, pointed at the dark shapes on the bed.

"What the hell's . . ." he began.

Gunn was on him in a flash. His right hand chopped downward while his left shot out and grabbed the back of the gunman's neck. The pistol clattered to the floor.

Soo Li stopped screaming. She cowered in the corner, her veins jellied by fear.

Gentry was strong. Gunn tried to put him under, driving a right into his ribs, but the gunny twisted away, broke free of Gunn's grasp. Gunn staggered forward, victim of his own furious momentum, clutching empty air. Seconds later, a fist crashed into his side, knocking his breath from his lungs. He fell to his knees, turned in time to ward off a savage swipe from Gentry's fist. The blow grazed his shoulder and he tumbled backwards, the gunman on top.

He grappled with Gentry. Gentry pumped a knee at Gunn's groin. Gunn rolled. The knee thudded into his thigh with bone-crunching impact. He pulled on Gentry's arms, flipping the man over on his back. Gunn was on him, hands reaching for his neck. He grabbed the man's chin insteat, forced his head backward. With a mighty effort of will, Gentry gathered both legs up close to his belly and lashed out. His stockinged feet caught Gunn at the belt line, lifted him up in the air, breaking his grip.

Gunn landed with a *whump*.

Somewhere on the dark floor, Gentry's pistol lay begging. Gentry scrambled for it as Soo Li cried out a warning. Gunn recovered, stretched out his length, grabbed his captor by the ankle. He pulled the man toward him as he struggled to get his feet under him. Gentry turned and kicked at Gunn's face. Gunn grabbed the other foot, rose up and gave a wrench of his arms. Gentry's body twisted and he was rolled onto his face. Gunn bent one leg at an angle, trying desperately to break it.

Soo Li crept cautiously along the wall. Reaching the door, she disappeared through it. In the next room, she searched frantically for matches and a lamp.

Gentry kicked both legs free, got to his feet. The two men circled each other in the almost pitch darkness, two silhouettes stalking each other with clenched fists. Gunn shot a probing left at the gunny's chin. Gentry avoided it easily, the fist swishing by his face in the darkness. He danced around Gunn, quick, lithe, flicking out his own fists. Gunn had the reach on him, began wading in, trying to land telling blows on the man's midsection, bring his guard down. His fist thudded into a hard gut. He took a grazing knuckle on his cheek.

A lamp bloomed behind them from the other room, throwing light on the two figures.

Gunn cranked his right, shot it forward as Gentry changed direction. The blow snapped Gentry's head back. He staggered, winced in pain. Backpedalling, he fought back as Gunn pressed his advantage. Throwing overhand rights and lefts, Gunn drove the man back, but most of his blows landed on Gentry's upraised arms. The light grew in intensity as Soo Li stood in the doorway, watching the two men. She had Gunn's pistol and knife cradled in her arm.

Gentry spotted his own pistol on the floor, dove for it.

His hands grasped the butt as Gunn hurled himself at Gentry, landed on his back. The two men rolled over and over, but Gentry raised the pistol. Gunn's arm stretched out, trying to reach it before the man could bring it to bear. Gentry rammed two quick lefts into Gunn's solar plexus, knocking the wind from him. Gunn's eyes blurred with pain. His lungs burned as if a match had been thrown down his throat. He gasped for air.

Gentry's hand was slick with sweat, but he quickened his grasp, brought the pistol around. His finger slipped inside the trigger guard.

Gunn scooted around, trying to get on Gentry's blind side. The gambit worked. Gentry fired the cocked pistol. The powder burned Gunn's cheek as an orange flame speared past him but the slug ripped into the wall. Rising quickly, Gunn kicked hard at Gentry's face. His heel smacked into the side of the gunman's head. Pressing his advantage, Gunn sprawled for the pistol before Gentry could recock it.

They struggled for possession of the .45. Gunn got both hands around Gentry's right wrist and hammered the man's hand against the floor until his fingers loosened around the grip. Gunn lunged for the pistol. Lights exploded in his brain as Gentry smashed a fist to the back of his head. Gunn rammed backward with an elbow, striking the gunny in the chest. Gentry grunted as the wind was knocked from his lungs. The pistol skittered away from Gunn's grasp, but he chased after it.

Hands clawed at his back, trying to drag him back. He kept on until his fingertips touched the pistol butt. He kicked one leg backward, connecting with Gentry's groin. The man let out a savage oath and groveled with pain.

Gunn's hand closed around the pistol grip.

Whirling, he swiped at Gentry's face. The barrel cracked against the man's temple. His pale blue eyes froze for an instant, then rolled backward in their sockets.

Gentry fell over like a sack of oats.

Gunn rose painfully to his feet.

Soo Li rushed into the room, the lamp bobbing in her hands. Gunn saw his shadow thrown against the wall, saw it waver like some caped night demon. He drew a full breath, closed his eyes. Steadied himself. He ached all over, his muscles sore from the pounding, the exertion. Every nerve end seemed to clamor in his brain.

"Who is he?" he gasped.

"Bud. He works for a man named Jason. They—they brought me here."

He took his holster and gunbelt from Soo Li, strapped them on. He emptied Gentry's pistol, tossed it into a corner of the room. He felt the lump on his head. He wished now he'd worn a hat when he left the hotel. It might have soaked up some of the blow. The gun butt hadn't broken the skin, but the bone was badly bruised. Otherwise, he was not badly hurt. Nothing was broken.

"Let's get out of here," he said.

"You should kill him," Soo Li said quietly.

He looked at her then. Her dark beauty was something to behold. The lamplight threw her face into relief, the taut skin, the high cheekbones, the almond-shaped eyes. She had the body of a young girl, but in her face there was wisdom, the wisdom of the ancients, hundreds of generations of Chinese lore and philosophy.

"I should, but I won't kill a defenseless man."

"He will try to kill you. He is cold. In his heart."

"Come on," he said, "before he wakes up."

"At least tie him up. This man is like a cat. He makes no sound. I have heard him talk with the Jason man. He is a killer."

Gunn knew she was right. Quickly, he lashed Gentry to the bed. He didn't regain consciousness. Gunn put on his boots, closed the door to the bedroom.

Soo Li blew out the lamp and they left the cabin.

Buck was still saddled. He helped Soo Li up, seated her behind the cantle.

He debated whether to wake Jilly up, have her keep the Chinese girl with her. That would be exposing her to unnecessary danger. He decided that it would be best if he kept her with him until he could make arrangements to get her back to Dixon. He could keep an eye on her, make sure that neither Berryman nor Gentry found out where she was.

The hotel clerk was asleep when the two sneaked into the lobby of the hotel. Quietly, they tiptoed up the stairs. Jilly's note was inside his room. She was in room number sixteen. He stuffed the note in his pocket, lit a lamp. His hat was on the bed where he had tossed it earlier. He moved it, turned back the covers.

"You sleep here," he said. "I'll take the bedroll on the floor."

Soo Li looked at him with a bemused smile. He turned his back while she undressed. Tomorrow he would have to buy her clothes.

"Are you decent?" he asked.

Soo Li giggled.

"I am in your bed," she told him.

He turned around, saw that she had the covers drawn up to her chin. Her clothes lay neatly folded on the chair. He spread his bedroll out on the floor, blew out the lamp. He undressed down to his shorts in the dark. He crawled into his blankets, wishing he could have taken a hot bath to soothe his aching muscles.

"Good night, Soo Li. I'll see that you get home safely."

"I know. You are a good man, Mister Gunn."

He closed his eyes, turned over, suddenly weary.

"Good night," said Soo Li, a few moments later. But Gunn was already asleep.

Warm flesh pressed against him.

He swam upward through cloud layers of sleep.

At first he thought he was camped out under the stars, that some furred animal had crawled into his bedroll. His mind cleared and he reached out a hand. Touched soft hair. A face. Nose. Lips. A delicate chin.

Jilly?

Where in hell was he?

It was still dark, but moonlight shimmered through the curtains. A soft breeze blew them into the room. They looked like fluttering ghosts, added a dimension of unreality to his surroundings. It took him several moments to get his bearings, realize he was in his own hotel room.

A mouth grazed his cheek, light as a feather.

He turned, felt soft hands touching his face. Warm legs against his.

She kissed him. He felt his loins heat with a sudden rush of sensation.

"Soo Li?"

"Yes."

Hungry lips sought his. He felt her hand at his scrotum, fingernails dancing on the wrinkled skin, crawling up to the base of his cock. Tiny breasts pressed into his bare chest. Kisses burned into his lips. Her tongue slithered into his mouth. He felt his manhood growing as her fingers closed around it, stroked it to throbbing life.

"You good man, Mr. Gunn. Soo Li very grateful. Make you very happy."

"You're just a kid, Soo Li."

"Soo Li is woman. I owe you my life."

Her breath was hot on his face. Her hand burned into the flesh of his cock, grown hard with the driven blood.

"You don't owe me anything," he husked.

"Oh, yes. Soo Li always repay her debts. My father taught me this."

"Your father would wring your neck if he knew."

She giggled in the dark.

"Soo Li very naughty girl."

She laughed again, crawled over him. Lean thighs pressed against his. She smothered him then with kisses, peppering his face, his lips, his neck with moist lips. Whatever resistance he might have had was quickly melted as Soo Li showered him with affection.

He touched a breast with his hand. Taut, spongy. He stirred the nipple with a fingertip.

Soo Li squirmed against him, hungry mouth roaming over his flesh. She seemed possessed of an overwhelming eagerness, a passionate desire that belied her years. He wondered if her sheltered life, her subsequent kidnap, hadn't ignited hidden tinders in her heart. His hand explored her young body, the flat tummy, the thatch between her quivering legs. When he touched her sex, she wriggled wildly. She flooded his hand with warm juices.

"Did Gentry . . ." he wondered.

"No," she breathed. "No man has touched me until now. He—he treated me with contempt."

So she had been scorned by the outlaw. And she was a virgin. He would never understand women, what drove them. Soo Li was a flower ready to be plucked and Gentry had treated her like a piece of meat. There were men like that. They looked at the surface, never beneath. Soo Li was desirable. Eager. She wanted him.

Now he wanted her.

He held her still, kissed her hard on her mouth. Her body stiffened, then shuddered as an electric spasm coursed through her. He forced her away from him, rose up with her in his arms. He carried her to the bed, laid her gently down. She waited for him, trembling legs spread wide. He slid atop her, entered her slowly.

She gasped. Sighed. A tight little elfin, her sex gripping him like a fisting hand as he slid inside. Her juices oiled his passage, drenched him in steamy velvet. He sank into the bubbling pudding of her, struck the leathery barrier of her maidenhead. She winced and he withdrew. Her arms wrapped around his wide shoulders. She pulled him to her, her hands frantic as they dug into his flesh.

"Please, Gunn," she whispered, "all the way."

"Soon," he said. "It's better if it happens slow."

He stroked her slow, the tip of his manhood striking the hymen, weakening it, relaxing its grip on her virginity. She arched her back as climactic spasms shook her body. She cried out like a lost kitten as the tough tissue guarding her love tunnel weakened, gave way. He waited until she was relaxed, then rammed home, searing through the membrane, burrowing past. Her scream was soft in his ears. He kissed the grateful tears on her cheeks, pressed his mouth to hers as he stroked deep through the bloody oils.

"Soo Li very happy," she breathed. "Thank you, Gunn. For making me woman."

"You already were, Soo Li. Nobody noticed, that's all."

"You sweet man, Gunn."

When he peaked out, flooding her with his milky seed, she exploded into a frenzy of joy. Her thighs clamped against him, her fingers dug into his shoulder blades. Her pussy squeezed him dry with spasmodic contractions of hidden muscles.

They slept long, past daybreak, close as two spoons in a drawer.

The knocking jolted them awake after the sun had filled the room with gold light, dancing motes of glittering dust. Soo Li clutched him, fear clouding her dark eyes.

CHAPTER THIRTEEN

Jason rode the big black, puffing on a cheroot.

Long before he reached the cabin, he sensed something was wrong. Bud wasn't out on the porch whittling as usual. There was no sign of life around the cabin. Except that Bud's roan was saddled, tied to the hitchrail, swatting flies in the midmorning sun. Either Bud had been out riding and just returned or he had left the horse saddled up all night. If Bud was a drinking man, that theory would hold water, but he wasn't. Perhaps, though, he had reverted to his old tricks and gone into town to earn some extra spending money.

Jason's jawline tautened. He didn't want Bud to foul things up now. His own situation was bad enough considering what had happened that morning. He had taken Amy into town, returned the rented buggy, saddled his horse. Amy had gone to the bank, promised to meet him with the money in a half hour or so. He had changed clothes at the hotel, met her at the restaurant.

"I have some bad news, Jason," she had said. "My bank account is low and I've got a payroll to meet. I'm having funds transferred from Missoula, but it'll take a couple of days."

He had tried to remain calm. His smile was forced, but he didn't want her to know how he felt. A delay in such matters was often a stall. Time gave the "mark" a chance to squirm out of the deal. Amy would have time to think now. She might begin to wonder why he couldn't have the local banker arrange for a transfer of his own funds or negotiate with the bank that supposedly carried letters of credit from the Chicago investors. There were a lot of flaws in his scheme, he realized. It was one thing to speak of money after making love to a woman, when she was basking in the glow of romance, and quite another to discuss finances in the cold light of day. The longer he delayed in getting the money from Amy, the less likely she was to believe in him. After all, he was borrowing a considerable sum. And his reasons for borrowing it were that he needed it in a hurry and he wanted to marry her right away. If the money was late in arriving, she would soon see through his scheme.

"My deal might fall through. I'm supposed to close the deal today. For cash."

"If you have fifty thousand, perhaps the seller will settle for a short-term note for the balance."

Jason had thought fast.

"I told you, Amy. There are other bidders. The man doesn't have to wait for his cash. No, I'm afraid I might have lost the deal. Couldn't you borrow the balance from your bank?"

"They're in the same position I am, Jason. They would have to get funds from another bank. I already asked."

It had been an effort to laugh, but he managed. There was no use pushing it.

"I'll see if I can't get the party to wait another two or three days. Thanks, Amy. If I lose this deal, though, I'm afraid my financial partners would replace me. It would be some time before I could recoup and think about marriage."

He had left it at that. The hook in, festering. If Amy bought it, he would be all right. If she didn't, he was out time and money. He had paid two hundred dollars for the ring, had lavished gifts on her, spent money on dining, drinks, lost some on bad cards. He still had a sizeable stake left over from Jilly's money but he needed more—much more.

Jason approached the cabin cautiously. He tossed his cheroot away and drew his pistol. He rode around the cabin once to make sure no one was skulking about. Then he dismounted, tied his horse to the hitchrail and walked up to the porch. He stepped carefully. Boards creaked underfoot. The silence was eerie.

He opened the door. The hinges squeaked.

"Bud?"

The front room was empty. Bud's boots lay by his bed. The door to the back bedroom was closed.

"Bud?" he said more loudly.

"Jason," someone rasped. "In here!"

Jason opened the door cautiously. The room was a shambles. His mouth dropped open when he saw a dazed and groggy Bud Gentry tied to the bed. Jason cursed, holstered his pistol, rushed to untie his erstwhile partner.

"What the hell happened here? Where's the Chink?"

Sheepishly, Bud told him of the events of the previous evening. He told him about Amos Dunbar's visit, the speculation that "Miss Smith of San Francisco" might be Jilly Collins. He related how he had seen the buckskin horse and had proceeded on foot to find a big man peeking through the window. He explained how he had coldcocked the stranger, tied him up with Soo Li and how they had tricked him.

"I'm sorry as hell, Jason, you know that."

"Did you ask the man's name?" Sarcasm oiled Jason's words.

"Thought we'd get it out of him this morning."

"Fat chance." Jason did not try to conceal his disgust.

"Dammit, Jason, they tricked me! Twarn't my fault!"

"I wonder how much that jasper heard out there. The bastard! Spying on Amy and me!"

"You figger it was that Gunn feller?"

"Who else? Fits the description. Same man I saw eyeing Amy at Stillman's last night." Jason walked to the front room, scratching his chin. He stuck a fresh cheroot in his mouth, lit it. Bud came in, slipped on his boots. He was raw hungry but he wanted to hear Jason out. Something was in his craw and he felt blamed bad about letting himself get fooled by a Chinee gal and a stranger. He made up his bunk, sat on it, waiting for Jason to continue the conversation. He sat there, then remembered his pistol. He went back and picked up the cartridges Gunn had strewn on the floor when he emptied Bud's cylinder. He found the pistol in the corner, reloaded it. When he got back in the front room, he strapped on his gun belt. He wished now he had just killed the man and been done with it. He sure was four kinds of fool for letting those two get away.

"Bud, I been thinkin'. You did good. Real good. At least we know what we're facing. You stopped that bastard from spying on me and while I would have killed him outright, you did what you thought was best."

Bud was pleased. A faint smile seemed to take some of the vacancy from his eyes.

"I'll kill him the next time I see him," Gentry promised.

"Yes. It may come to that. The way I figure it, this character's got something up his sleeve. Maybe he's sweet on the Collins gal. Or maybe he's just hiring out to her. She's been dogging my trail ever since I left St. Louie and that's because she wants her money back. Well, we're still a jump ahead of 'em."

"Yeah?"

"Yeah. Jilly's probably at the hotel. She doesn't know that we know that. This Gunn feller is playing some kind of game. He hasn't made a move. Just skulking around, spying on me. Now he's got the Chink. So what? She's no longer useful to us. Just a liability. All I have to do is play a close hand. What room's Jilly in?''

"Amos said number sixteen.''

"Good. Now Jilly doesn't know what you look like. Here's what I want you to do.''

"Gunn! Are you there?''

Gunn's stomach turned queasy.

Jilly!

He put a finger to his lips as Soo Li stared at him questioningly, her sloe eyes wide.

"Just a minute, Jilly!''

Things would be a mess in just a few minutes if he didn't think fast. Damn Jilly! He had told her to stay in her room. But she was pounding on his door, waking up everybody. Mainly him. And Soo Li was as naked as dawn.

He looked down at his own nakedness. The bedroll on the floor. The rumpled bed. Soo Li gawking at him with those inpenetrable eyes. It was a hell of a note.

"Get under the bed,'' he whispered to Soo Li. "I'll take care of it. It's, uh, a friend.''

He sensed the Chinese girl's disapproval. He leaped out of bed, grabbed her clothes up, tossed them on his bedroll, rolled it all up and shoved it against the wall. Hurriedly, he climbed into his own clothes, went to the door. His shirt was unbuttoned; he was barefoot.

He opened the door a crack.

"Jilly, what are you doing here?" he whispered.

"I'm hungry," she said loudly. "Let me in."

"Uh, well, Jilly, I, uh, ah, just woke up and . . ."

She shoved him aside imperiously, strode into the room.

"Now, Jilly, listen, I can explain—it's not what you think."

He looked quickly at the bed. Soo Li was out of sight.

Jilly looked around the room, her suspicions aroused.

"What's going on here?" she asked. "You're acting very strange."

"Strange? Me?"

"Gunn! Are you drunk?"

"Yeah. A little. I mean I was out late last night. Overslept. Jilly, look, you go on back to your room. I'll get some grub, bring it up to you."

"I've already eaten."

"You what?"

"I got tired of waiting and went down to the restaurant. It's just down the block."

"Are you crazy? Jason could have seen you."

"Jason isn't here. He's registered at the hotel, but he's not in his room. While you've been out gallivanting all night, getting liquored up, I've been trying to find out where Jason is with my money. I thought you came along to help me." She stood there, eying him accusingly, her legs spread apart. He noticed, then, that she wore a hat with a veil stuck on the brim. A prim dress, high-heeled shoes. It was no disguise, but she looked fetching, he had to admit.

"Jilly, I can explain. Just let me get dressed, shaved. I—I'll see you in a while." He started to push her out of the room, but she wouldn't budge.

"You're trying to get rid of me, Gunn. Why? Are you expecting someone?"

"No!" he said quickly. Too quickly. "I—I'm not expecting anyone. I've got a lot to tell you, Jilly. Where Jason is, who's working for him. A lot."

"You're as nervous as a bridegroom, Gunn." She looked around the room, sniffed the air. Her eyes went to the rumpled bed. She saw the dark stains on the sheets. Dried blood. Or chocolate.

Gunn mentally kicked himself. He wished he could shrink to the size of a mouse and scurry away, out of Jilly's accusing sight.

Jilly walked over the bed, hips swaying. She leaned over it, examining the tell-tale stains.

She whirled, her eyes flashing.

"Are you hurt?"

He rubbed the lump on his head.

"A little. I got conked on the head last night."

"Ooooh, let me see."

He backed away.

"No, it's all right. Please, Jilly, you—you shouldn't be here."

Her suspicions were aroused again.

"You're hiding something from me, Gunn." Pause. "Were you shot?"

"Naow. Dammit, Jilly." He stood there, defeated by her persistence.

Underneath the bed, Soo Li's nose twitched involuntarily. Dust from the floor drifted into her nostrils, tickled the tiny hairs inside. She drew a finger up to her nose, trying to stave off a sneeze. The silence in the room was deafening.

Jilly eyed Gunn, noted his obvious discomfort at her presence. He looked down at his naked feet. Moved his toes. He wished he were any place else but where he was.

"Uh, uh, uh, uh, uuuuuuuuuuhhhhhhhaaaaaaaaaa-ah CHOOOOOOOO!"

Jilly jumped a foot, frightened out of her wits.

"My god, what was that?"

"Oh, shit!" exclaimed Gunn.

Jilly whirled, dropped to her knees by the side of the bed.

She peered into Soo Li's fawn eyes. Soo Li blinked at Jilly. Jilly's mouth gaped open.

Gunn stood there, squirming. He brought a hand to his face, rubbed his eyes. He was having a nightmare in broad daylight.

"Who are you?" demanded Jilly. "Come out of there."

A frail and naked Soo Li crawled out from under the bed. She stood there, next to Jilly, her breasts, legs and tummy smeared with dust. She sneezed again.

Jilly jumped backward.

Gunn laughed.

Soo Li looked penitent. But she was not embarrassed. Gunn looked at her admiringly. Jilly glared at him, put her hand on her hips.

"Maybe you'd better do some explaining, *Mister* Gunn. Who is this girl? What is she doing in your room?"

"Soo Li woman."

"Soo Li? Why, you're—you're Hop Chee's daughter!"

"She is," grinned Gunn. "Now why don't you sit down, Jilly, and I'll tell you all about it."

"Soo Li get clothes."

"In the bedroll, Soo Li."

Jilly softened toward the girl, but she continued to glare at Gunn. Well, the cat was out of the bag. He led Jilly to a chair while Soo Li rummaged for her clothing. Jilly jerked her arms away, huffed to a chair, sat stiffly.

While Soo Li dressed, Gunn told Jilly everything that had happened the night before. Everything except what Jilly most wanted to know.

"And so that's all of it, Jilly. See?" He grinned at her idiotically.

Jilly sat silent, fuming with unsaid words, unanswered questions.

Soo Li bowed, fully dressed.

"Gunn saved Soo Li's life. Gunn is good man. Soo Li very grateful." She overpronounced her Rs.

"Yes, I'm sure Soo Li is grateful," Jilly said icily.

"Well, I'm powerful starved," Gunn said. "Guess me and Soo Li'll get something to eat." He bent over to get his socks and boots. Jilly rose from her chair and kicked him squarely in the butt. Gunn went sprawling, fell spreadeagled on the floor.

Soo Li tittered girlishly.

Jilly, seeing the comic aspects of the situation, finally, threw back her head and laughed.

She put her arm around Soo Li's waist. Together, they laughed at the disheveled Gunn who crawled for his footing.

"I'm glad you're safe, Soo Li," Jilly said. "And you're right. Gunn is a good man. A damned good man."

CHAPTER FOURTEEN

"So," said Gunn, "it's my belief that Jason will do everything he can to keep any of us from spoiling his romance with this Amy woman. She seems to have money. From what I learned this afternoon, she owns the Rawlings Freight outfit, Stillman's and a restaurant. I figure Jason is out to skin her for all he can get."

"Why don't we just face Jason down, demand the return of my money?" Jilly asked.

Gunn stretched out his legs. Soo Li sat on the bed, curled up like a kitten in her new clothes, her calves tucked under her thighs. She had braided her long black hair into a single strand, bathed and scented herself. Jilly sat on the other chair in his room, dressed in a new outfit, as well. Two beautiful woman. If not friends, then envious sisters sharing the same beau.

"I'm going to face Jason down," said Gunn. "In my own way. Publicly."

"Why?"

Gunn took a deep breath. He had thought about it a long time. From what he had observed, Jason Berryman was a swaggering, cocky, self-centered man, very impressed with his own importance. He was also a rogue and a scoundrel. A base man who preyed on helpless women. Such a man brought shame to every man. As long as he was allowed to use his wiles against females, allowed to get by with taking advantage of women's weaknesses, no man was safe from condemnation, censure. He was no better than a common thief. The West was full of men who were worse, but there were none lower in character. Berryman didn't kill. So far. But he robbed women of much more than money. He robbed them of self-respect. He took their love, their devotion and stamped it underfoot, ground it into a manure pile.

"Jilly, when you married Jason Berryman, it was in a public ceremony. All of your friends were there. You were happy. Proud. Then the man took your money and left you. He humiliated you publicly. Is this not so?"

"Why, yes, I suppose."

"Then, if you believe in justice, let me handle it. I want everyone to know what kind of man this Jason is. I want to call him out in front of his friends."

"But . . ."

"Wait a minute." Gunn put up a hand. "Let me finish. I want to bring Jason down in front of the woman he's wooing now. Amy Rawlings. Is that not justice?"

Jilly hopped from her chair, planted a kiss on Gunn's forehead. His forehead turned a rosy hue.

"Oh, Gunn, you're beautiful! Of course! It's perfect!"

"Hey, Jilly. Hold on. I said that's what I plan to do. There's no guarantee."

"You will do it, Gunn," said Soo Li, breaking her silence. "You can do anything."

Jilly laughed. Gunn smiled at Soo Li.

"There's one other matter we have to consider," said Gunn. "This one is more serious."

Jilly sat down, willing to listen now to all of Gunn's plans. Soo Li shifted her position on the bed. She stretched out her lean legs, draped them over the edge. Her tiny feet were encased in satin slippers.

"What matter is that?" asked Jilly.

"Bud Gentry. Soo Li has told me some about him. I still have a sore spot on my skull from the man. My hunch is he'll be smarting from having the tables turned on him. He'll come hunting someone. Me, you, or Soo Li. Or all of us. And, he won't wait. From what Soo Li said, I'd say he'll make his move tonight."

Jilly gasped.

Soo Li nodded sagely.

"And when he does," said Gunn, "I want to be ready for him. So here's what we're going to do . . ."

Bud Gentry slashed at the pine stob with his Barlow. Slivers of soft wood fell to the porch. A bird called somewhere in the hills. The sun hung there on a peak, boiling red flame.

He'd had a bellyful of waiting. His nerves were jangling like a wagonload of Mexican spurs. Every time he thought of how that sonofabitch had suckered him, a knot tightened in his gut. He'd like to take the pocketknife and make a coin purse out of that mother-humpin' bastard's nut bag.

Still, maybe Jason was right. Stay away from Gunn. Concentrate on the girl. He didn't hold with hurting a white woman. That was the surest way to get killed. He had argued about that with Jason for a whole quarter hour. A Chinee gal was different. No man would say much about her. But the white woman was another matter. There were lines you didn't step over and that was one of them. If a woman wore pants, that was one thing. Most men in the West got terrible riled up if a woman put on a man's pants. Like Jason said this Jilly gal did. Woman who wore pants was considered downright peculiar. Women belonged in dresses and that was that.

Jason said he didn't have to hurt the Collins gal. Just be polite to her, get her out to the cabin where he could talk to her. If she came quiet, all right. If she wanted to raise a ruckus, let her look into the business end of a .45 for about thirty seconds. If she still didn't want to go, then wait her out. Use her as bait for Gunn. He comes in her room, blow his lights out and the gal's too. Let the story be told that Gunn and Jilly Collins had a real serious lover's quarrel and their tempers went to triggers. Happened all the time. Him? He was just tryin' to recon—reconsigh, jest tryin' to patch things up a'tween 'em.

If it come to that, and he had to shoot them both, Jason would step forward and tell about how the woman carried a pistol, wore a man's clothes and had been loose of morals. He would admit he had married her and found out about her afterwards. It was a slick story and he had to hand it to Jason. He had brains. He could sure think of things neat and tidy like that.

Jason was going to stick pretty close to the Rawlings woman. He didn't want to give her time to think about the money. The die was done cast and in a couple of days they'd be riding west with all that money. Jason said he'd asked for $10,000. He'd keep a third for expenses, a third for himself and give a third to him. He didn't know what a third was until Jason said it was $3300. Hell, that was more money'n he'd ever seen all at once't. That was mighty fair of Jason to include him in the deal. If a woman was gullible enough to give that kind of money to a man, why, he reckoned she didn't deserve it nohow.

The sun finally slipped over the peak, gilding it with a shimmering frame.

Bud always felt better when the sun went down. More like himself. He slowed down his whittling, becoming calmer as the shadows stretched out, thickened. He cocked his head, figured his time. Dusk wouldn't do it. He'd have to go into town when it was almost pitch dark. But the timing was even more crucial.

After supper, but before the Collins woman took

a hankerin' to step out for some night life. That is, before she started lookin' for Jason at the card tables. Amos Dunbar was going to leave a key to her room in an envelope at the desk. For a "Mister Barlow." Hell, that was downright funny. Another smart thing Jason thunk up. Usin' the name of his knife for an alias.

There was only one question in Bud Gentry's mind as he prepared to ride into the settlement.

He wondered, if it came to killing the Collins woman, if he should get another grizzly tooth for his necklace.

Gunn sat in Jilly's room, looking out the window.

He was alone.

The falling sun turned the sky to peach. The undersides of sheep clouds glistened like pearls for an instant, then turned purple deepening to blue-black, finally turning to ash, darkening to dead coals.

Jilly and Soo Li were in his room.

Jilly was armed.

He didn't think anyone would come to his room. There was no lamp lit in his room. Nor would there be. He had left specific instructions. The lamp in Jilly's room burned bright, throwing, he knew, a slice of yellow light under the door. A beacon in the night of the hotel corridor.

Someone would come, he was sure.

An extra key to Jilly's room was missing. The clerk had asked her about it earlier. "Did she have the extra key?" She did not. The evening man, Will

Parsons, had offered to move her to another room. He couldn't understand why there wasn't a spare key in her message box. Gunn knew why. Someone had taken it. The usual evening clerk, Amos Dunbar, who was conveniently "off" this evening. Off and establishing an alibi, most likely.

Gunn hoped that it wouldn't be Jason.

It wouldn't be. Jason Berryman would not soil his hands. He, too, would be establishing an alibi. He'd be courting Amy Rawlings publicly. Well, he would get to him, in due time. In public. He hoped Amy Rawlings would be with him. She should know what kind of man he was. Everyone should know.

The night deepened. The silence in the room was the silence of a cave. And he was the dweller in that cave. Waiting. Waiting for something that might not happen.

Gunn believed in hunches, however. Hunches had saved his life more than once. Hunches were like glimpses into the future. A man didn't get them often, but when he did, he should treat them as a gift. Respect them. Act on them. Woman called such occurrences by the name of intuition.

Indians believed in it. So did animals. Gunn, when he was a boy growing up in Arkansas, had seen a deer, downwind, using the same trail it had used for days, suddenly stop, and for some unexplainable reason, take another path, out of range. No scent, no sound, no sight had changed the buck's mind. Only intuition. A feeling. A hunch.

Footsteps jarred Gunn from his musing.

He tensed in the chair. Sat perfectly still.

The footsteps paused, continued on down the

hall. Had they stopped in front of Jilly's door?

There was no way to be sure.

He heard a key rattle a lock. A door opened. Closed.

The silence returned.

Seconds ticked by, slow as honey chilled in a spring house.

Outside, in the dark, a mother called to her young son to come inside. The boy protested. The mother threatened him with a thrashing. More argument. A man's voice called out the boy's name. Billy. The boy said he was coming right home. A dog yapped, then howled in pain. Someone had either kicked it or thrown something at it.

A door opened on the same floor of the hotel.

Two women's voices drifted to him. They were old, chattering about a meeting somewhere in the settlement. Their footsteps passed by without stopping. Silence drifted back on the heels of the fading footsteps.

Lights winked in the darkness. From somewhere far off he heard the faint strains of a hurdy gurdy. Laughter snatched away by the night breeze like smoke from a campfire.

He heard no footsteps.

Just the metallic scrape of a key going into the door.

Gunn's hand dropped to his gunbutt. He slipped his .45 out of the holster as the key turned in the lock.

The door would open inward. Whoever was there would have to step into the room. Gunn's chair was placed to one side, next to the window. He would have first look.

The tumbler clicked back. The key was still.

The door handle turned. Slick and quiet.

Gunn brought his pistol up, ready to hammer back.

The door swung open. A foot and a half. Stopped.

Gunn heard the controlled breathing. A board gave where the man shifted his weight. It was only a slight sound, hardly noticeable.

Gunn held the pistol loosely in his hand. His elbow was bent, the pistol perfectly balanced. No strain on his muscles. Thumb poised next to the hammer.

The door opened another six inches.

Bud Gentry stepped inside the room, pistol drawn.

Gunn's thumb flicked out. The hammer pulled back, cocking the pistol.

"Drop it, Gentry. If it don't fall straight down when you open your hand, you'll follow it to the floor."

Gentry took several seconds to decide. Gunn's pistol didn't waiver. He had Gentry cold and Gentry knew it.

The pistol dropped just like Gunn had ordered it. Straight down as Gentry opened his hand.

"Step lightly into the room. I want to see both hands in plain sight while you do."

The gunman glided into the room on cat feet. Gunn wondered how he did it.

"That's far enough." Gunn rose from his chair. He circled Gentry, kicked his pistol away from the door, closed it with his foot. He came up from behind, put the barrel of his Peacemaker into the small of Gentry's back.

"Stretch your arms straight out, chest high."

Gentry did that.

Gunn went over him, looking for a hideout pistol, a knife. There was only the pocketknife. He left it there.

"What's your play, Gunn? I reckon that's who you are."

"I'm Gunn. I ask the questions. Where's Berryman?"

"I don't know."

Gunn rammed the barrel against Gentry's kidney. The man winced all over.

"P-playing cards, I reckon. Down to Stillman's."

"Step over to that table yonder. Put your hands flat on the top."

Gunn's pistol prodded him over to the table. Gentry leaned over, lay his hands out flat.

"You right-handed or left-handed?"

"Right-handed."

Gunn stepped around him.

"That's what I figured," he said, bringing the butt of his pistol down hard on the fingers of Gentry's right hand. There was a sickening crunch of tiny bones.

Gentry screamed in pain. Gunn jerked the hand back to the table, came down hard again. Bone shattered again as the butt smashed into the back of Gentry's hand. Gentry dropped like a stone, unconscious.

Gunn jerked him up by his shirt front, tapped his

face with the gun barrel. Hard enough to jar the man back to consciousness. Gentry's right hand hung from his arm, began to swell. His face contorted in pain.

"Now, I reckon we'll go down to Stillman's you and me, and play a little cards. You play cards, Gentry?"

CHAPTER FIFTEEN

It was a long walk down to Stillman's for Bud Gentry.

Gunn had unloaded his pistol, shoved it back in the holster, "So's you won't look too unnatural," and told Gentry to walk two paces ahead. "If you try to run, you'll be wolfmeat before you get two steps. Powder burns pretty fast these days."

Gentry held his swollen hand up high with his good hand. The hand had turned a sickly color, puffed up as if he'd been snake bit. At least he was alive. Once again, Gunn had suckered him.

His pale blue eyes blazed with hatred while his gut fluttered with fear and humiliation.

"Step inside, Gentry," Gunn said affably when they came to Stillman's bat-wings. "I'll buy you a drink, then let you go on home. I see you on the streets again, I'll air you out with lead pills. Give you a gut ache'll make you think that hand is soaking in warm salts."

Jason's face fell when he saw Bud Gentry come into the saloon, Gunn a step behind him. His look of dismay changed to puzzlement as the two walked over to the bar. There was something odd about Gentry. His face was white as a ghost and he seemed to be carrying something in his hands.

Jason sat at a poker table with five other men, facing the door.

Amy Rawlings was nowhere in sight.

Gunn made no sign he knew Jason by sight. He gently nudged Gentry up to the bar.

"A pair of whiskies," he told the bartender. "Go ahead, Gentry, and rest your hand on the bar. A little painkiller won't hurt none, will it?"

"Fuck you, Gunn," Gentry said under his breath.

"Aw, now. Is that any way to talk to a man who's buying you a drink?" Gunn put money on the bar. He turned so that Gentry would have a good look at his right hand, his holstered pistol.

The bartender served the whiskies, took the money. He appeared not to notice Gentry's hand, but everyone at the bar did. No one said anything. It was best not to ask questions of strangers. None of them had ever seen Gentry before, but they could see he needed medical attention.

"Just what in hell do you want, Gunn?" Gentry whispered, his voice hoarse with anger.

Gunn raised his glass, took a quick sip.

"I want you to ride that roan horse of yours right out of town and as far as you can go. Don't look back. Don't even think about it. You get one free drink for your trouble."

"That all?"

"Oh, one more thing."

"What's that?" Gentry downed his drink in one gulp. Tears watered his eyes.

"God help you if you're left-handed."

Gentry walked toward the bat-wing doors. Jason's eyes followed him. Gentry turned slightly, held out his swollen hand. Shrugged. Jason's eyes narrowed.

Gunn watched the exchange, a slow smile spreading from his lips.

Jason's eyes flicked to Gunn.

Gunn brought two fingers up to his hat brim. Grinned.

Jason scowled.

Gunn finished his drink, sauntered over to the table where Jason was playing.

"Got an opening," he said coolly, "I'd like to set with you gentlemen."

One of the men looked up, heaved a sigh. He had a very short stack of chips in front of him.

"You can have this chair, I reckon, unless I fill this straight."

"Thank you kindly."

Jason glowered, but said nothing. A few seconds later, the man scraped his chair back, stood up. He hadn't filled his straight.

"Twenty buy-in," Jason said coldly. "No limit, three raises."

Gunn bought a hundred dollars worth of chips. Might as well announce his intentions right off.

"My name's Jason, this here's Clem, and Pike, Lefty, Tom."

"Call me Gunn."

Jason's eyes flickered. He lit a cheroot. His hands were steady as he struck the sulphur match.

"Your deal, Pike," said Clem, passing the cards to him. Jason and Gunn faced each other. Clem was on Jason's left, then Pike. Lefty and Tom flanked Gunn. They were men in their forties, ranchers, Gunn gathered. Shopkeepers generally were too smart and careful with money to frequent gambling saloons. Cowhands were too poor to play with professionals like Jason. There was well over a thousand dollars worth of chips in the game and Gunn reasoned that it hadn't been in progress long. The men all looked too fresh, too relaxed. They smelled of bay rum and whiskey. Lefty was drinking beer. Clem smoked foul-smelling cigars. Tom drank coffee, was more neatly dressed than the others, a shade older.

The bartender took drink orders. Gunn ordered another whiskey. He didn't want to lose his edge. He was pleased that he had been able to take Gentry out of action. He had stopped briefly at his own room, told Jilly what he was going to do. He hadn't let Gentry get a look at her. He wanted the women to stay in his room until he returned. Jilly wanted to know what he was going to do, but he hadn't told her. She was impetuous. She was liable to come down to Stillman's and face Jason despite the danger.

As they played, Gunn took note of Jason at close range. The man was shrewd, cool, steady of hand and eye. He was a good poker player. The game was honest, friendly. Gunn pressed some hands to test the mettle of his playing companions. Mainly he wanted to see how Jason handled himself. No one made any reference to Gentry. No one asked Gunn where he was from, what his business was. The others talked of sheep and cattle, mentioned the Indian trouble over in Oregon and in the Black Hills country. Some allowed as it was settled, others said that uprisings would continue as long as there was an Indian on his home grounds. Gunn stayed out of the talk, watching, waiting.

Jason was winning. The pots got sweeter. More money came into the game. Gunn's stack grew slowly. He played poker only occasionally. Liked the game. He had learned it more to find out about men than for any other reason. He usually did not like to spend so much time indoors, idling away precious time. But, upon occasion, he found it useful to play cards, frequent the saloons. A man could often pick up valuable information in such places, at such pastimes. Like now.

After an hour, Jason began to glance up from his cards every now and then. Make a quick sweep of the room with his eyes. Gunn thought he knew why.

He was looking For Amy Rawlings. So far, she had not put in an appearance. Jason was casual about looking for her, but the edges of his eyes betrayed his growing nervousness. Gunn smiled inwardly. Likely Jason was wondering if he had gotten to her as well as Gentry. But Amy Rawlings did not fit into his plans, except that he was going to do her a big favor if he could pull it off.

He tried to conceal his disgust for Jason Berryman. The gambler's oiliness disgusted Gunn. The slicked down hair, the pomaded moustache, the neatly trimmed sideburns, the impeccable black suit, white shirt, string tie. The pistol always visible inside his coat, snuggled up belt high. Like a gentleman would wear a gun. The pistol was formidable enough. It was a Remington .44, a conversion. One of the new model Armys. A man like Jason was likely to have a

Derringer tucked away in some handy place, as well.

A half hour later, Amy Rawlings came into the saloon. From the back hallway. Either she had just come in to town, or she had been going over the books in her office. She looked fresh and sparkling, ravishingly beautiful. Gunn's eyes flickered over her ample body, the bulwark of her bosom. She wore a black dress, the breasts rimmed by lacy frills, mounds of flesh peeking through. She wore a velvet choker, an ivory cameo hanging just above her cleavage. She gave her greetings to the bartender, the men at the bar. Ordered a drink. Champagne, Gunn noticed. She saw him, finally, and her eyes widened in surprise. Jason smiled wanly at her. He shot a dark look at Gunn, who kept his face neutral as best he could.

"Good evening, gentlemen," Amy said, coming up only when the current hand was dead, Jason raking in the first pot in the last ten he'd won.

"Good evening, Miss Rawlings," chorused the players.

"Hello, Amy," said Jason smoothly. "I don't believe you've met our newest player. Gunn, this is Miss Rawlings. Your hostess here at Stillman's. She owns the place."

"Oh, Jason, you needn't have said that. Let Mr. Gunn enjoy himself. Are you enjoying yourself, Mr. Gunn?"

"I am. And there's no mister in front of the

name, begging your pardon, Miss Rawlings."

"Gunn? You're not the one I heard about over in Virginia City, are you. The one the miners all talk about?"

"I wouldn't know, Miss Rawlings." It was Gunn's deal. He picked up the cards, shuffled them quickly.

"Good luck to all of you," Amy said, smiling. She began to circulate around the room, saying hello to friends. She sat down with some men at one table, laughing and joking with them.

But her eyes kept coming back to Gunn's. There was respect and puzzlement in her glances. Gunn began to concentrate on the game. Now that Amy Rawlings was here, he was ready to make his move. He had the money to back his play.

He hoped he had the nerve.

Bud Gentry had no intention of leaving the settlement. He wanted that $3300 Jason had promised him.

He also wanted to kill Gunn.

Now, more than ever.

His hand was plumb crushed. It throbbed with pain, looked like he had stuck it in a hornet's nest and give 'em the fuck-you sign for ten minutes. It was all swolled up twice't its size. No way to set any of the little bones until the damn thing shrunk back to its regular shape. And that would take a while for sure.

After leaving Stillman's, Bud had gone to the

place where his roan was tied. Two doors down from the hotel behind the Golden Elk Restaurant. Now, he stood in the shadows, shoving cartridges into the cylinder of his .45. At least he had that. If push come to shove, he could shoot left-handed. Have to steady his hand some, but it was possible to plug that sonofabitch in the back. And that was the onliest way he was ever going to get the drop on that uncanny bastard Gunn. The man had second sight, for sure.

He had heard of men like Gunn. The Mexicans called them *hombres de sombra*. Men of shadow. But there was no equivalent in English. Unless you called the shadow by the name of Fate. The Mexes believed that some men were guided by a kind of shadow-ghost. This shadow not only followed a man, but led him.

Gunn was an *hombre de sombra*, for sure. If you believed in that adobe bullshit.

Bud didn't want to believe it, but Gunn had him spooked.

Sometimes, the Mexicans said, the shadow fell asleep. At such times, the man was in danger. Well, he damn sure meant to stalk Gunn, push him to the limit. Get him when his shadow was asleep.

He finished loading the pistol. No empty cylinder. Six bullets. He held the pistol in his left hand, practiced aiming, cocking. Easing the hammer back down slow while the barrel was pointed at the ground. Awkward, but he could do it. His right hand hurt something fierce, but if he concentrated on his anger, his hatred of Gunn, some of the pain went away. He would feel the blood pulsing in the swollen tissue, though. It was like a heartbeat, as if he had a heart attached to his wrist.

Bud worked his gunbelt around so that the pistol rested in the holster, butt out, on his left hip. He practiced drawing from that side. The first few attempts were clumsy, but the technique worked after he got used to the position of the pistol and holster. He had to twist his left wrist to draw, once going for the pistol butt, and again after he pulled the weapon free of the holster. He would win no quick draw contest, but he could get the pistol out fairly fast.

Besides, he wouldn't have to outdraw Gunn.

All he had to do was get Gunn to come to him.

And be waiting for him.

Amos Dunbar lived in a small room at the back of the hotel, downstairs. The room was free, part of his salary as a clerk. He was twenty-six years old, with muddy brown hair, close-set brown eyes, a smooth face. He was a bachelor because he was an introvert. He read adventure books and dreamed of becoming what he wasn't, a brave man, a hero. Like others, he had come west to seek his fortune, but the west had beaten him down. He found no gold, only meanness and disappointment. He didn't realize that he found the things that were in his heart. He expected to be disappointed and he was. He did not believe, completely, the stories of rich gold strikes. He looked for meanness and he found it. Somehow, he drifted west until his fear of the unknown became too great and he would go no farther. So, he stayed in the settlement, got a job as evening clerk at the Coeur d'Alene.

The only excitement he'd known had been when rich men stopped at the hotel. And lately, he had enjoyed the extra money given to him by Jason Berryman. Enjoyed playing the spy, being, for Mr. Berryman, at least, important.

For giving the key to Bud Gentry, and bringing the message about "Miss Smith," Amos was richer by twenty dollars. He understood there would be more in a few days. For services rendered. He liked Mr. Berryman. He was very generous and he was courting the richest woman in town, Amy Rawlings. Just knowing him made Amos feel important.

He was lying on the bed in his room, arms folded behind his head, dreaming of being rich and famous, when the knock came.

"Hello, Bud, come on in. What happened to your hand?"

"A little accident. Amos, Jason wants you to do a job for him. Won't be much."

Amos beamed. Bud didn't look good. His face

was wan, his hand looked like a bloated animal that had been skinned and boiled.

"What?"

"Just go upstairs with me. I want you to knock on number 14. Two women in there. Miss Smith and a Chinee girl. You tell 'em you got a message for them from Gunn. They open the door, you step aside quick."

"I dunno, Bud." Amos scratched the back of his head. "I told Mr. Berryman I didn't want to get personally involved."

Bud Gentry drew his pistol. Pretty fast. He cocked it, shoved it into Amos' belly. Amos turned pale. His eyes seemed to cross.

"You'll do it, Amos, or I'll spill your guts right here. You are involved. Right up to your eyeteeth."

Sweat broke out on Dunbar's brow.

He would do what Bud wanted. After he changed clothes.

Amos Dunbar was a coward.

His bladder emptied, staining his trousers with steaming urine.

CHAPTER SIXTEEN

Gunn was making some enemies.

He made it costly for the other players in the game. When he opened, he sucked them all in with ten dollar bets. After the draw, he bet heavy. He made it steep to stay in and try to draw him out. By betting heavy after the draw, he began to wear the other players down. They had no stomach for playing with a wild man who was also lucky.

The problem was to keep Jason in the game, while driving the others out.

When Jason had a good hand, Gunn let him ride it out. It was tricky business. If he overdid it, it would look as if he and the oily gambler were in cahoots.

Tom had gotten cleaned out early.

That left Clem, Pike, Lefty and Jason facing Gunn's reckless betting.

Clem was stubborn. It cost him dearly. Gunn got him with a high flush. Clem stayed in all the way through three outrageous raises of two hundred dollars each, then winced as Gunn turned his cards. All red. All hearts. Queen high.

"Too rich for my blood," said Clem, sliding out of his chair. No mention of luck. Or anything liable to be taken wrong.

The crowd sensed the energy in the game. A low hum of conversation began to rise from the other tables.

Amy Rawlings kept her eyes on the play, but stayed well away. Jason was holding his own, so she wasn't worried. Not yet.

More people came into the saloon as word spread around town that a stranger was putting the quirt to the heavy bettors, making them hump it and run for cover. Whispers in the saloon itself were of the consensus that there was some blood between Jason Berryman and the man called Gunn. No one had as yet put a word to it, and no mention was made of collusion. It was just a feeling that everyone had. A gut feeling.

"Anyone else want in this game?" asked Pike, scratching his beard. He looked around the room. A lot of heads shook vigorously. "Well, I'm going to see how the money goes for a couple more hands, then scout myself up a barrel. You boys play real hard."

"That supposed to mean something?" asked Gunn. Politely.

"Not a thing, Gunn. Just watchin' them chips is

like watchin' a horseshoe game. They go back and forth, always 'tween the same two posts.''

"Bring in a fresh deck," Jason said, breaking the tension.

Someone brought up a card press, passed it around. The cards often curled, since they were made of uncoated paper, and were kept in a press, a box with a screw down against a block of wood, so that they could be kept usable for a longer time.

"You pick out the deck, Pike," Gunn said. "See if your luck won't change."

Pike cracked a new deck, took out one joker, shuffled. Jason cut. Lefty opened. No raises. Everyone stayed. Gunn went in with two pair, discarded the odd card. Lefty took two cards, Pike three and Jason one. Lefty bet fifty dollars after the draw. Gunn bumped him three hundred. He caught a jack, giving him three to go over the pair of nines. Jason called, raised five hundred. Pike dropped out, disgusted. Lefty called, but Gunn raised another five hundred. Jason called. Lefty called.

He was low man with three sevens, a pair of eights full. Jason had a full house, too—three tens, two aces. Gunn pulled in the pot.

Pike lasted a half dozen more hands before he was cleaned out.

Jason, Lefty and Gunn continued playing.

Amy Rawlings drifted over between hands to give Jason encouragement. He was holding his own, but Gunn was nibbling away at his pile. Lefty was getting nervous. The pots were all running over $1000 a hand and there was between $5000 and $10,000 in chips on the table. Lefty's greed kept him in. He started chasing his money, trying to bluff Gunn. Gunn didn't buy it and managed to drive Lefty up against the wall.

By then, everyone in the saloon knew that the duel was shaping up between Jason and Gunn.

They sensed the tension between the two men.

Gunn was relaxed, calm, affable.

Jason was oily, reserved, visibly cool. Only a faint twitching at the corners of his eyes betrayed his apprehension.

"You two know each other before?" Lefty asked Jason.

"Never saw the man in my life," said Berryman.

"That's right," said Gunn, his pale gray eyes boring into Jason's.

Lefty seemed satisfied, but baffled by the murderous raises, the almost eerie luck of the two men. Still, he took the cards for his deal, anted in ten dollars. Gunn drew an ace high flush on a pat hand, made known his intentions when he opened.

"Open for five hundred," he said evenly.

Jason did not blink an eye, but called.

Lefty folded. "I'm out after the deal," he said. "You two want to buck heads, you don't need me."

Jason took a card. He had gone in with four cards to a king high spade flush. He drew a fifth spade, a deuce. Gunn bet a thousand. Jason bumped a thousand. Gunn raised back, Jason called.

"Sonofabitch!" someone exclaimed when Gunn spread his heart flush on the table.

172

"All the way to the ace," said Gunn.

"Beats mine," said Jason, forcing a smile.

"Here, Gunn," said Lefty, "you win the deal too."

"Miss Rawlings," Gunn said, looking into Amy's cobalt eyes, "I'd like to buy the house a drink." He reached in his pocket, brought out a wad of bills. Everyone stared, including Jason. There were a few low whistles, some raucous cheers.

Jason's eyes widened. Gunn had as much as insulted him. Besides that, the man had appealed to his greed. His fingers fidgeted. He wondered if he could get away with dealing seconds. He looked around him. No, too many people. Someone with a good ear would likely spot him. He was confident enough of his dexterity to pull it off visually, but a keen listener could hear the telltale *click* when the lower card slipped out. No, Gunn couldn't be beaten that way. He didn't know what the man was trying to prove, but he sensed that matters were coming to a head. If he left the game now, everyone in there would wonder why. Worse, Amy would lose respect for him. She might even begin to fishtail out of the loan.

Drinks were poured and passed. Gunn rolled a quirly, lit it. He finished the whiskey he had ordered when he first sat down to the game. Someone brought him another. Good stuff. None of that head-buster rotgut that passed for drinkin' whiskey in one-horse towns. He tasted the fresh drink, smacked his lips.

"Old Crow," said Amy, coming up behind him.

"You owe the bar forty dollars."

Gunn gave her a hundred.

"Let them run this out," he said.

"Are you and Jason through playing?" she asked.

"No, I think we're just beginning, aren't we, Jason?" His smile was wide. The challenge had been laid down.

"That's up to you, Gunn. Time limit?"

"No. Five card stud. No limit. Hundred dollar ante."

"Suit yourself." Jason clicked a stack of chips together as he lifted them up, let them fall through a cone of fingers.

Amy eyed the two, consternation darkening her freckled face.

"Good luck to both of you," she said. But there was a warning for Jason in her eyes. She, too, sensed that there was something between the two men that was not visible to the casual observer. There was an undercurrent of energy that flowed between them. She shuddered, despite herself, then left them, taking the money to the bar.

The talk died away as a fresh deck was brought. Jason shuffled, Gunn cut. Jason dealt. By calling the game, five card stud, Gunn had made it into a spectator's game. A ring of people crowded around to watch the two men buck heads.

Gunn figured Jason had three or four thousand in chips. Maybe a few hundred more in his pockets. He didn't know how the hands would fall, but he had played tight all evening. None of his bluffs had ever been called because he made sure the first few times he came out strong that he had a hand to back up his bet. But the circumstances were different now. In a stud game, you could only bluff your hole card. And if he got caught, Jason would gobble him alive. Still, it was his game and the money moved faster since bets went down on each showing of the cards. He didn't want anyone to lose interest. He wanted to put Jason against a wall and then put the spur to his flank. He wanted Jason to buck and buck hard.

Gunn played loose, for a time. He played on Jason's greed. The chips flowed back and forth, but Jason was ahead. And gaining. That was the way Gunn wanted it. He watched the cards carefully, watched the way Jason's greed took hold. He let himself get caught bluffing. Once, twice, a third time. Jason began to enjoy himself. He leaned over the table, winked at Amy. He was going to skin this cowboy St. Louis style.

"Let's up the ante," Jason said finally. "Say five hundred?"

That's what Gunn had been waiting for.

"Why not a thousand?"

Jason smiled, tweaked his grease-thickened moustache. He winked at Amy. Slyly. Amy smiled her encouragement.

"A thousand it is," said Jason, snaking out a cheroot. Amy lit it for him, rubbed his shoulders. When she leaned over, Gunn stared at her creamy breasts. His pale eyes danced with merriment.

"I'm going to enjoy this, Gunn."

"I hope you do, Mr. Berryman."

It was Gunn's deal.

Jilly paced the floor nervously.

Soo Li looked at her, wondering when she would explode.

"Where is he?" Jilly spat. "Where in hell *is* he?"

"You must be patient, Jilly. Do you want to talk some more?"

It seemed to Jilly that they had talked for hours. She had told the Chinese girl her life's story, had listened to hers. They both had avoided talking about Gunn. But he was right on the edge of their conversation, in their thoughts.

"No. I'm worried now. Jason might have killed him!"

"Would he do that? Could he?"

"Oh, I don't know, Soo Li. I—I'm just worried, that's all." Jilly wrung her hands in anguish. She stopped pacing, flopped in a chair. She drew her dress up, exposing her thighs. The small pistol was strapped to one thigh. She looked at it, stroked the pearlhandled butt. "I ought to go down there, see if Gunn is still alive. Or just shoot Jason."

"Is it the money you want so much?"

"No, not anymore. I—I think I'm falling for Gunn."

"You love him?"

"I don't know, Soo Li. After Jason, I never thought I could trust another man. But Gunn's different. The way he looks at me. The way he looks on a horse. I can't get him out of my mind."

Soo Li fell silent. She looked down at her lap. The bed moved as she swung off it, came over to kneel before Jilly. She took her hands, rubbed them gently.

Jilly looked into Soo Li's sad dark eyes.

"Do not worry about Gunn. He is a very special man."

"You love him too, don't you, Soo Li?"

Soo Li turned away, looked out the window, into the night.

"I don't know. Soo Li does not want to hurt you. Or be hurt."

Jilly was interrupted by a cautious knock on the door. She rose from the chair. Soo Li rose, too, but restrained Jilly.

"Let me go," said Jilly impatiently. "That's probably Gunn . . ."

"No," Soo Li whispered. "It is not Gunn. Be careful."

The knock came again. Slightly louder.

"Who is it?" called Jilly.

"It—it's me, the evening clerk, ma'am. Amos Dunbar."

Jilly advanced toward the door, shaking off Soo Li's grip around her wrist. She hiked her dress up, and slipped the little Colt Third .41 out of the holster.

"What do you want, Mr. Dunbar?"

A pause.

"Message for you, ma'am."

Jilly knew then that the man was lying. This was Gunn's room. The only way he could know she was in there would be if he was in cahoots with Jason.

"Give me the message."

Another pause. Jilly heard whispers.

"It's wrote down, Miss Smith."

"Slip it under the door."

Another pause, more whispers. Jilly moved to the side of the door, cocked the pistol.

"A package with it, ma'am. And I got to deliver it personal."

"Just leave it outside, Mr. Dunbar."

"You got to sign. Cain't leave it, 'less you sign for it, ma'am."

Stalemate.

Jilly bit her underlip. She looked wild-eyed at Soo Li. The Chinese girl shrugged, shook her head. Her skin was pale.

"Just—just a minute," Jilly said, stalling.

She had two shots in the Derringer. Gunn's Winchester leaned against the wall. Loaded. Someone was out there with Dunbar. They wanted in. It could be Jason. If so, that probably meant that he had killed Gunn. Or had him killed. Quickly, she tiptoed over to Soo Li, handed her the cocked Colt. She pointed to the door, gestured, her hand shaped like a gun, her finger pulling an imaginary trigger. She picked up Gunn's rifle, stepped back to stand five paces in front of the door.

"Who's the message from?" she asked.

There was no answer. Instead, there was the sound of a key being rammed into the lock.

Jilly cocked the Winchester as the handle turned, the door burst open.

CHAPTER SEVENTEEN

Percival Merriwether finished dressing Abigail's arm.

"You heal fast for a woman of your maturity, Mrs. Evanston."

"My name's Abigail, Doctor Merriweather. Or you can call me Abby."

"Well, Abby, another day or two ought to do it."

Abigail reached out with her good arm and ringed the doctor's neck. She pulled his face to hers and planted a juicy kiss on his mouth. He sputtered, startled. Abigail hung on to him. She was sober, too.

"Percy, I want you to leave with me in the morning. To Cataldo Mission. I've done nothing but worry about that gal of mine. Now, don't say a word. I'll pay your way. I've decided to keep that covered buckboard and ride up there and surprise Jilly. In fact, I'd like to take you back to St. Louis with me when we complete our business out here."

She smacked him with another kiss, released him.

"You're a handsome woman, Abby. I'll give you that. But, I've a practice here in Dixon and . . ."

"Pshaw! I won't hear another flimsy excuse, Percy. You like me. I like you. Now, where's my prescription? We'll drink on it."

Merriwether reached into his bag, brought out the bottle of Old Crow. Abigail had stayed sober the past two days. They had shared a brought-in dinner the previous evening. He enjoyed her company. The woman wasn't as old as she sometimes looked and she had a style. That's what she had: pure style. He seldom saw it anymore.

He had been nothing more than a horse doctor back East. Then, the war came along and he had studied up, gotten his surgeon's license. Practical experience in the field had tempted him into a pretty good physician and cutter. After Appomatox, he had drifted West, to the gold fields, then settled for a more peaceful existence in the Mission Settlement. He would never become rich here though, and perhaps it was time to move on. Abigail had made him a very tempting offer. The truth was, he had been thinking of moving on to California.

He poured drinks for them.

"Would you consider going on to San Francisco with me, Abby?"

She cocked her head, eyed him with those hawk eyes of hers.

"Serious?"

"Serious."

"Well, now, I just might. You know I'm pushing fifty. Creaky in the bones."

"You appear to be a sound woman to me. And we're about the same age. If age is important to you."

"It ain't. Isn't."

"I think we could set up a good practice out there."

"You're a delicious man, Percy. Make me feel like a whole woman, even with this scratched wing."

"You are a whole woman, Abby."

She smiled warmly at him. The years dropped away from her face. It glowed. He leaned over, kissed her tenderly. On the nose. She squirmed like a schoolgirl.

"Will you go to the Mission with me?"

"I will. Have to come back here, though, and settle my affairs before we go on West."

She extended a frail veined hand.

"It's a deal," she said, shaking his hand. "Leave early in the morning."

He finished his drink, reached down for his bag.

"I'll get everything ready," he said, starting to rise from his chair.

"Percy, wait."

"What?"

"You don't have to leave just yet, do you? I may be an old gal, but there's still smoke in my chimney."

"I know there is, Abby. You want me to stay awhile?"

"I want you to stay all night. I have an alarm clock."

Percival Merriwether set his bag back down on the floor. Abigail tossed off her drink, scooted to the other side of the bed. She blew out the lamp. In the dark, there was a rustle of clothes as the doctor undressed.

Moments later the bed slats creaked as he crawled into Abigail's bed.

Amos Dunbar turned the door handle slowly. His hand was trembling.

Behind him, Bud Gentry held the .45 in his left hand, the barrel snug against Dunbar's kidney.

"Push the door open," Bud whispered.

"I—I can't." Dunbar's bladder was weakening again.

"You rather get aired out with a .45? Hell, they ain't but two little ol' gals in there, man."

Dunbar pushed the door open.

His eyes went wide as he saw Jilly Collins standing there, a Winchester in her hands.

Gentry shoved Dunbar ahead of him.

Jilly cocked the Winchester. The sound was sharp, deadly, as if someone had rung a guillotine to the top of its frame.

Dunbar cried out in fright.

Gentry tried to bring his pistol to bear. Awkwardly, he raised his left arm. He hadn't expected this. He wanted the two women alive. Now, the Collins gal had a Winchester cocked and aimed square at his head. His right hand throbbed like a wounded heart. It was in the way, a festering club that was as useless as teats on a boar.

Soo Li raised the small Colt. Her arm was shaking, but Dunbar saw the action and panic flooded his senses.

He whirled, scrambling to flee.

Gentry tried to avoid him, stepped to his right. His pistol boomed.

Orange flame belched from the barrel of his gun. Powder burned a streak across Dunbar's face. He howled in pain and crashed into Gentry's broken hand.

The bullet from Gentry's pistol whizzed past Jilly's head, blew out the windowpane. Glass shattered as she fired pointblank at Gentry.

Gentry screamed as his crushed hand smashed into his belly, forced there by Dunbar's headlong flight to escape death. A second later, Jilly's .44 bullet speared his shoulder, shearing off a slice of flesh, furrowing an ugly gray groove through bone and gristle. Blood sprayed from the wound. Bud's body twisted around. One leg gave way at the knee. He fell backwards, screaming from the hurt in his hand, not his shoulder.

Dunbar landed atop Gentry's shattered hand, adding to the pain.

Gentry flailed at Dunbar with his good hand, trying to knock him off.

The desk clerk, addled by fear, cowered, his hands behind his head, trying to hide. But Gentry was beneath him, pounding on him, screaming so as to nigh break his ear drums.

Jilly and Soo Li raced into the hall. Jilly kicked the pistol away from Gentry. She kicked Dunbar in the side, trying to knock him off Gentry. People swarmed into the hall, terrified, confused. They saw the two women with pistol and rifle, and scrambled back into the rooms, slamming doors. Someone went to get the sheriff, collided with the substitute clerk on the stairs. Bedlam reigned, but Jilly and Soo Li were composed, calm and sure in their handling of the situation.

Soo Li reached down and grabbed Dunbar by the collar, jerked him off the screaming Gentry.

Jilly cocked the rifle again, efecting the empty brass casing.

She shoved the snout of the Winchester in Gentry's open mouth.

"Get up slow, mister, or this hammer comes down."

"Jesus, lady," he screeched, "I'm bleeding to death. My hand!"

"You're in a bad way. Your own fault. Now get up."

Soo Li prodded Dunbar to his feet. Gentry had to make it on his own. He struggled up, fell back, but the pain was too great to stay in that position, so he edged to the wall and forced himself to stand. Dunbar shook in his shoes, stuttering unintelligible pleas for mercy from the Chinese girl who held the deadly single shot in her hand.

Jilly picked up Gentry's pistol, held it in her left hand, ready to cock.

The sheriff and a deputy stormed up the stairs, guns drawn. The evening clerk followed them, enormously upset.

"What's going on here?" asked the sheriff, a man named Butterfield. He took one look at Gentry's bleeding shoulder and dropped his jaw. He was as confused as Dunbar when he saw the two armed women holding two men at bay, one of them badly wounded.

As calmly as she could, Jilly explained her side of the story.

"This man tried to kill us. He shot and broke that window out there. I shot him in the shoulder. The desk clerk there was helping him break into our room."

"Lord gawdamighty," exclaimed the Deputy, whose name was Maxwell. "We got ourselves a couple of rapers here."

"Shutup," said Butterfield. It took him fifteen minutes to sort out the story. Gentry whimpered in pain the whole time. He was a sorry sight.

"You'll have to prefer charges, probably testify in court," Butterfield explained to the two women after getting their names. "Circuit judge won't be here for a month."

"I'll swear out an affidavit in the morning," Jilly said. "Now, if you would be so kind as to get these two scoundrels out of here, we'll be about our business. Here's this man's pistol."

The sheriff reached to Jilly's tone, took Gentry's pistol, and meekly ordered his deputy to help him get the two men off to jail.

After they had left, Jilly and Soo Li went back inside Gunn's room and locked the door.

Then Jilly broke down. She began to tremble when she put the rifle down.

Soo Li put her arm around Jilly's shoulder.

"God, I was scared," she said, fighting off hysteria.

"I was too, missy. Very fearful."

"I—I've got to get a grip on myself, Soo Li. I've got to find Gunn!"

"You want Soo Li to go with you?"

"No. The two of us would attract too much attention. Let me get my wits together. I'll dress prim and wear a veil so Jason won't recognize me."

"Where will you go?"

"To Stillman's. I think that's where Gunn is.

And probably Jason. I don't want him to worry. I'm sure the story of this incident will get around town pretty fast."

"You probably right, Jilly. We go to your room and change?"

"Yes. And I'll carry that pistol, just in case there's someone else that bastard Jason has hired."

"You talk like man sometimes," Soo Li observed with a smile.

"Sometimes I wish I were one, Soo Li."

"But you are woman."

Jilly looked at her tenderly. Kissed her impulsively on the cheek. She had stopped trembling.

"Thanks, Soo Li. For helping. I couldn't have handled that by myself."

"Soo Li think so."

"You know, I think you're right. Right now I think I could handle anything. We whipped those two men, didn't we?"

"Yes, missy. We whipped them good!"

Gunn shuffled the cards, shoved them across the table for the cut.

Jason cut twice, towards Gunn.

Gunn smiled.

"Cut 'em thin, bound to win. Cut deep, losers weep," he said.

"Just deal, Gunn. We can do without the homespun philosophy."

"Sure, Jason. I like a man who's anxious."

Jason frowned, annoyed by Gunn's cockiness.

Gunn shot him a hole card, dropped one for himself. He turned up a four for Jason, an eight on top of his hole card.

"Bet a thousand," he said, shoving chips out into the center of the table. "In the dark."

Jason looked at his hole card.

"Call," he said.

Next to fall on Jason's hand was a trey. Gunn drew a five. He bet another thousand, Jason called.

Jason got a five, Gunn another eight.

"Possible small straight," he said to Jason. "Pair of eights." He looked at his hole card then. A lone queen. He bet another thousand. Jason didn't raise. The last card for Jason was a six. Gunn drew a five. Two pair showing. He bet two thousand, Jason raised him two. Gunn called.

Jason turned over a deuce.

"Straight to the six," he said.

"Two pair," Gunn said.

Jason raked in the pot, grinning. Amy smiled at him warmly.

It was going his way. The chips tumbled from their stacks, spreading out in front of him. He felt fat. Gunn could be had. He would be had.

"Your deal, Jason," Gunn said amiably, gathering up the cards.

"Ante a thousand."

"Done and done."

Jason wondered why Gunn was so damned

smug. He had just lost seven thousand dollars and he was grinning like a Cheshire cat. Either he planned to cheat or he was just plain crazy. So far, he had detected no cheating, but Gunn was acting too damned smart-aleck to suit him.

Jason examined the deck, looking for shaved edges, pinched corners. Sometimes a gambler would mark cards during play and this would give him an advantage. The cards were clean, much to his surprise. He shuffled three times, offered the deck for the cut.

"Run 'em," Gunn said.

Jason's eyebrows went up.

He shrugged, began to deal.

No one noticed the small woman in the long dress who edged her way into Stillman's. She wore a long skirt of light tweed, a matching jacket, prim brown blouse. She also wore a cloche and her face was veiled. Brown gloves and matching brown shoes and handbag completed her wardrobe. She went to the far end of the bar, sat on a high stool, craning her neck to see through the crowd.

"Rye," she whispered to the bartender. "Water."

She put money on the bar.

"Who's playing over there?" she asked the bartender.

"Fellow named Gunn and Mr. Berryman. Buckin' heads. The Gunn feller's losing his a . . . er, not doing too well."

"Oh, I doubt that, mister," said Jilly. "I'll bet Mr. Gunn's going to do just fine."

CHAPTER EIGHTEEN

Jason threw Gunn a ten on his hole card.
Flicked himself an ace.

"Bet a thousand," Jason said. "In the dark."

His sarcasm was not lost on Gunn. He covered the thousand, let his hole card ride without a peek.

Jason skidded a king across the table to Gunn, another to himself. There was a fly-buzz of conversation that surged through the crowd. Both men looked at their hole cards. Jason felt fat. He had another king in the hole. Gunn looked at his hole card twice more. Jason resisted the urge to smirk. A man looked at his hole card that much was looking for it to change size and spots. He figured Gunn for a low card. Maybe a deuce.

Jason bet two thousand. A thousand for each king.

To his surprise, Gunn called.

Again, the crowd reacted. The whispers whicked through the room in an ebb and flow of speculative talk. Jilly Collins stood up on the stool so that she could get a better view. She saw Jason through the haze of cigar smoke, Gunn's shoulders, profile. She imagined his gray steel eyes, his sensuous lips, the lock of hair falling over his broad honest forehead. She wished she could go to him, tell him she was behind him. Her eyes fell on Amy Rawlings, narrowed. The woman was voluptuous, beautiful in an earthy, buxom way. She could see why Jason was attracted to her. She reeked of money and success, yet she was open, giving, honest. Why was it, she wondered, that the honest people were always easy victims of men like Jason Berryman? Yet it was so. She had not been able to see past his physical appearance, his cultivated charm. He was smooth, Jason was. Smooth and pretty, but he had no character. Not like Gunn. He might not have Jason's book education, but he was a much smarter man. He was more manly, even. Silently, she prayed that he would win, that he would best Jason. But from the bee-hive hum of talk, she knew that the crowd was pulling for Jason, that they believed he had already won.

"Thet Jase, he gonna clean that cheechako out," said a grizzled old-timer in the crowd.

"He too slick for the cowpoke, thet's fer sure," agreed his partner.

Jilly wanted to scream support for her champion, to tell them that they were wrong. She suppressed the urge and sipped the throat-slashing rye, taking courage from the glow in her stomach, the warmth flooding her veins.

Gunn looked at his hole card again. Deliberate, as if he was sweating out a mate or wishing it were something else. Jason noted that, once again. Gunn had never been overly concerned about his hole card before. Now he was. It was worth some thought. If he followed true to form, he had a bad one in there.

Jason held a pair of kings wired, with an ace kicker. The beauty of it was that his pair of cowboys wasn't showing.

He dealt the next two cards.

Gunn caught Jason's king. The crowd gasped.

Jason got a ten.

"Your bet," said Jason coldly.

"Check," said Gunn, quickly.

Too quickly, Jason thought.

He eyed the cards carefully. He didn't want to appear too eager. As it stood, Gunn showed a ten, a pair of kings. He, himself, had an ace, king, ten showing. His king in the hole gave him a higher hand than Gunn had showing. He knew that Gunn could have no more than two kings. He probably had a low card in the hole. By catching the ten himself, he raised the odds that Gunn would catch two pair higher than his. It was worth a bet into the check.

"I'll have to go to three thousand on a possible straight," said Jason. Words. Give him words. Let him chew on them, choke on them, throw them up like vomit in the last card. Lull the sonofabitch, nail him.

Gunn hesitated. Deliberate again. He counted his chips. Checked his hole card, the shadow of disgust crossing his face.

"Gettin' pretty steep," Gunn said quietly, letting his southern drawl laze over the syllables like creek water bubbling over stones.

"You have another card coming, Gunn."

"Reckon I gotta stay. I have some investment there, all right."

Isolated murmurs from the crowd. Nudges from surreptitious elbows. Sly smiles. Knowing winks.

Amy looked at Gunn's face, wondering what Jason read in it. She examined his smoky gray eyes, the sensual, almost cruel lips. A cigarette dangled from his lips, the fumes drifting off to the side of his cheek almost like the trace of a scar. His soft brown hat, slightly misshapen, was pushed back on his forehead, allowing a lock of his dark brown hair to fall over his brow. He needed a haircut. The ends were ragged, uneven, as if he had cut it himself on some lonely windswept trail, peering into a polished steel mirror. His vest hung loosely over his shirt. The shirt was open and curlicued hairs furred the muscles of his broad chest. She could read nothing on his face, in his eyes. Nothing but cruelty and passion and perhaps a kind of trail wisdom that was unfathomable to any but mountain men, cowhands and men who lived on the fringes of society, just outside the law. She felt, despite herself, something primitive and bestial stir in her loins, in her heart. Ashamed, she looked away, conscious that a flush had darkened her cheeks, made the freckles flare as they did when she was erotically aroused. She coughed, buried her head in her hands until the feeling passed.

Jilly noticed the Rawlings woman blush. She knew instinctively why. The woman had been staring at Gunn, staring hard, and her lust had surged to the surface. It was a fleeting moment of startling insight. Jilly felt a twinge of jealousy, a pang of regret. If all women felt that way when they looked at Gunn, what chance had she to capture his heart?

Gunn counted out the chips, reluctantly pushed them into the center.

"I'll call one more time," he said. "Do me

196

good, Jason."

Something like a sigh of relief sobbed through the crowd as if someone had started pumping a giant bellows.

Jason sucked in a breath. Gunn dropped his cigarette to the floor, ground it out with his heel. He seemed tensed for the next, and last, card.

Gunn caught a ten on his last card. His features scowled in disappointment. He did not look at his hole card.

Jason dropped the second ace into his row of cards. A pair of aces showing, but Gunn had two pair, kings and tens, on the board.

"Hell, if you got it in the hole, you probably got me beat," said Gunn. "But I have to bet you my two pair."

Jason said nothing. His face masked his inner elation. If Gunn bet into his blind two pair, Jason could clean him out. That would send Gunn on his way, his tail tucked between his legs. He would do his gloating after Gunn lost his shirt.

"You're high," Jason said.

Gunn gave everyone the impression that he was thinking out loud.

"Still," he said, "you might have a third ace tucked down in that hole. Or another ten. Maybe a king. Gives a man pause, for damn sure." He stacked his chips, separating whites, reds and blues. Whites were ten dollars, reds were hundreds, and blues five hundreds. Everyone in the room watched him count the chips. Not once, but twice. Jason licked his lips.

"If you're worried, Gunn, then check," Jason prodded.

"Oh, I'm worried all right. I think you been pushing me to the fence all this game long. And that worries the hell out of me. I got practically my whole hand out here showing and it looks mighty good. But you may have come in with aces wired for all I know. That last ace out there is looking pretty fierce about now."

"Bet or check," Jason said coldly, sure now that he had Gunn against the wall.

"No limit, right?"

Someone coughed.

Some warning flicker leaped in Jason's eyes.

"No limit, Gunn." There was a smug note in Jason's tone.

"Well, then," said Gunn, reaching inside his vest to his shirt pocket, "let's see here." He pulled out a sheaf of papers, bank drafts, letters of credit. He shoved all of his chips into the center of the table, tossed the money, bank drafts, papers, on top of the pile.

"What's that?" asked the incredulous Jason.

"I bet forty thousand dollars."

Jason gasped.

"Forty thousand dollars? Where in hell did you come up with that figure?" He riffled through the money, the drafts and letters of credit. It was a truly awesome sum.

All conversation died out as if someone had shut off the bellows, sucked all the breath out of every single person in the saloon. The silence around the table deepened like a gathering pool of dangerous water around bathers in an ankle deep stream.

"That's the amount you suckered your wife Jilly out of back in St. Louis. Jill Collins. Name ring a bell, Jason?"

Jason's face went bone white.

Amy looked at her lover, deeply puzzled. Jason stared at Gunn, a look of total shock on his face. Gradually, the look changed to a scowl of hatred.

"Are you going to call my bet, Mr. Berryman?" Gunn asked quietly.

Jason looked down at the pile of chips and paper. He looked sick. Everyone who was close enough to see locked their eyes on Jason's face. Jason stared like a man who has suddenly discovered a rattlesnake in his soup bowl. His mind raced frantically. If he backed down now, he would lose everything. Everything. The money, Amy, perhaps his freedom. He could not afford to back down. Besides, he had Gunn cold. He had a king in the hole. A higher two pair than Gunn had. Showing, anyway.

Jason saw everything clearly now. Gunn had made is move. The one he came in to Stillman's to make. It had nothing to do with poker. He had meant to expose Jason from the beginning, meant to cause him trouble with Amy. Well, it just wouldn't work. Gunn had nothing to back up his claim. All Jason had to do was deny Gunn's claims and that would end the matter. But first, he had to beat him at poker. Pin his ears back and strip him of his bankroll.

"You talk pretty free, Gunn," Jason said. "I'm not married and I don't know anyone by the name you mentioned."

"You don't have to call."

Jason looked frantically at Amy.

"I—I'm going to call you, Gunn. You aren't going to buy this pot."

There was a quick series of gasps from several in the crowd.

"Put your money out there, or your note, Jason."

"I—I don't have that much on me. Nor in town, either."

"How much you got?"

"Twenty thousand."

"Not enough. You gypped a good woman out of forty thousand."

Jason blanched again.

"Amy? Can you cover me?"

Amy glared at Gunn, certain that he was trying to buy a pot he didn't deserve. If he'd had the cards, he would have bet small, Jason might have raised, and he'd have been chased. By betting such an outrageous amount he was advertising the fact that he had only what was showing and hoped Jason had none better.

"Let me see your hole card," she said. "That all right with you, Mister Gunn?"

"It's your money, if you back him."

Amy walked around the table, dipped down to peer at Jason's hole card. She breathed a quick sigh of relief when she saw the king.

"I'll back your bet," she said. "Somebody get me a piece of paper."

Jason fished in his pockets, brought out a thick wallet. He counted out enough to make twenty thousand with the chips he had in front of him. Amy signed a note, tossed it into the pile.

"I want Jason's signature on that note, too, ma'am," Gunn said. "No offense. But he's the one owes the forty thousand."

"I don't believe you!" snapped Amy Rawlings.

"Oh, hell, I'll sign the damned note," Jason said, anxious to cut off the exchange between Gunn and Amy. Someone handed him a pencil. He signed hurriedly, tossed the note back on the table.

"I'll want that cash on the barrelhead if you lose," Gunn warned.

"Tomorrow," Amy said. "No later."

"Fine."

"I called you, Gunn," Jason said arrogantly. "Show us your hole card."

"I thought you was a mite prouder of yours, Mr. Berryman. You first."

Confidently, Jason turned up his king.

The crowd hummed with satisfaction, smirked with pleasure.

Amy swelled up proud.

"At least let me see the card I paid to see," said Jason. "Looks like your two pair didn't hold up."

"Nope, you're sure right about that, Jason. They didn't hold up. Fact is, I don't have two pair at all. Not anymore."

Jason's face registered disbelief.

Amy's eyebrows arched.

Gunn turned over his hole card. The third ten!

"Full house," he said bluntly. "Tens over cowboys."

Jason gasped audibly.

The crowd sucked in its breath in unison.

"You godamned tinhorn!" Jason rasped.

Furious, he snatched his note up from the table, shoved back with his chair and kicked out with both feet. His boots struck the table, lifted up and dumped it on Gunn. Jason swirled out of his chair, drew his pistol and fired pointblank where Gunn should have been behind the table. The pistol roared as smoke and flame spewed from its barrel. There was the angry thud of the ball splatting into wood, ripping splinters.

Then Jason ran through the crowd.

Amy screamed. Gunn scrambled free of chips and table. Splinters lodged in his vest, but the bullet had missed him.

"Stop him!" Gunn said, his pistol in his hand. But Jason was gone.

CHAPTER NINETEEN

The crowd held Gunn back.

He tried to fight through them. Finally, when they realized he was armed, they parted, but Jason had run out the back and was nowhere to be seen.

The crowd thinned further as he came back to the center of the saloon where Amy Rawlings waited, fuming like an overboiled pot.

Before he reached her, he was accosted by a veiled woman. He tried to sidestep her, but she kept blocking his way. It finally dawned on him that he knew who it was.

"Jilly?"

"Yes. You were wonderful, Gunn. Too bad that scoundrel got away." She lifted her veil. Gunn holstered his pistol, took her in his arms. He hugged her. She hugged back.

Someone gathered up the chips and money in his hat. The man was a bowlegged mountain man, long of beard, red of eye.

"Here ye be, stranger. Reckon you won that hand. Cain't rightly say what kind of game you were playin', but ye handled yourself mite pert."

"Thanks, old-timer. This your hat?"

"Wuz, wuz. I reckon you need it more'n me."

Gunn laughed, gave the man twenty dollars. "Buy yourself a new one," he said. He put the banknotes and papers back in his shirt pocket. The chips stayed in the battered old hat. Gunn wadded it up, stuck it inside his belt.

Amy Rawlings came up, eyes blazing.

"What's all this about? Who is this woman?"

"Miss Rawlings, may I present Miss Jill Collins. Formerly Mrs. Jason Berryman." Gunn stepped back, a grim half-smile on his face.

"You're a liar!" snapped Amy. She glared at Jilly.

Jilly's temper flared. She stepped up to Amy and slapped her hard across the mouth.

"Why you little bitch!" Amy screeched, her hand rising to her face. Red streaks marked where Jilly's hand had landed. Stunned, it took her several seconds to recover. When she realized that everyone was staring at her and that Jilly was within range, she exploded in a fury. Her hands reached for Jilly's hat. Fingernails caught in the veil and she jerked the cloche from Jilly's head.

"Yipe!" Jilly yipped as hair fasteners, holding her hat in place, pulled strands of hair from her scalp.

"I'll teach you to belt me!" Amy exclaimed, clawing at Jilly's face.

"Ladies!" yelled Gunn, trying to separate them.

Amy forged ahead, arms flailing. She caught Gunn in the temple with a raking hand. He staggered backwards, as the two women locked hands, wrestled for position.

The crowd spread wide, giving the two women a circle in which to do battle. Cheers for the favorites rose up.

"Smack her Amy!"

"Look out, Jilly!" said a man who had heard her name.

Bets were laid down as factions were formed.

Jilly was the odds-on underdog.

Still, Gunn tried to break it up. To his sorrow.

Amy grabbed Jilly's hair, pulled on it while Jilly yowled in humiliation and pain. She kicked out just as Gunn rushed in to try and stop the donnybrook. Jilly's knee caught him square in the scrotum. He doubled up in agony and rolled away from the action, cursing under his breath. He felt as if he'd been hit with an axe handle. The pain shot up into his groin. He touched a hand there to see if one of his testicles had been driven out of its sac. No, it was just a shooting pain as if a boil had been lanced with a cold pick.

Meanwhile, Jilly and Amy were doing their best to annihilate each other.

Jilly managed to grab Amy's hair, pulling out tufts of it. Amy screamed like a wildcat dipped in turpentine. She clawed Jilly's bodice, ripping her jacket downward. Enraged, Jilly counter-attacked, tearing the lace from Amy's dress, then wrenching half of the bodice away. One of Amy's bulbous breasts fell out of her brassiere. She punched Jilly in the solar plexus, knocking the wind from her.

"Five dollars says Amy beats the pants off the little lady!" shouted a man leaping to a chair.

"Covered!"

"Ten dollars on the little wildcat in brown!" said another.

"You got it!"

"Stop it, dammit, stop it!" Gunn husked. His voice couldn't be heard above the uproar. And he stood there, hunched over in pain, hoping his testicle would return to normal size. It seemed to be as big as a grapefruit. And it throbbed like the end of the world.

Jilly connected with a straight uppercut to Amy's chin. Amy's eyes crossed and she backpedalled, as Jilly waded in, swinging. The crowd surged apart to give them fighting room.

Amy recovered and whacked Jilly in the mouth, splitting her lip. Blood coursed down her chin. Undaunted, she grabbed the bodice over the unexposed breast and jerked hard. Amy's other breast tumbled into view. Unaware of this, Amy kicked Jilly in the shins.

Jilly kicked back, landing a shoe against Amy's thigh, driving her off-balance.

Pressing her advantage, Jilly leaped on Amy's back, clawing and smashing with tiny balled fists.

Amy yelped like a kicked dog. She spun around in circles trying desperately to hurl the monster from her back. She staggered to her knees, fell down. Twisting, she grabbed Jilly's collar with both hands. She tugged and the jacket ripped in half. Amy then grasped the woman's blouse and splayed it in two. Jilly's black brassiere hung on her shoulders by a single strap.

Amy tried to smash Jilly's breasts, but Jilly rolled and fought back wildly.

The crowd went insane.

Men's eyes popped from their sockets.

Gunn gave up trying to stop it and started betting on Jilly.

"The hell with it," he said. "No one's going to get those two gals apart unless one of them dies."

Someone slapped him on the back. He gave two to one odds on Jilly and started to pray.

Over and over the two women rolled and

tumbled. It was impossible to assess who was winning. Amy's eye was puffed up. Jilly had a lump in the center of her forehead. Her lips stopped bleeding, but there were angry red scratches on her neck and shoulders. She was now bare to the waist a was Amy.

The two women then began to work on each other's skirts.

They shrieked vile insults at each other, turning the already thick air in the saloon plum blue.

Finally, Jilly managed to get atop Amy and pin her back to the floor. She then grabbed her by the ears and started pounding her head on the sawdust-strewn floor. Amy's eyes rolled in their sockets. Her tongue lolled out.

"Stop the fight!" someone yelled. "Declare the little lady in brown a winner."

Two men grabbed Jilly's arms, jerked her away from Amy. Amy sat up groggily, her pendulous breasts soaked with sweat. She looked up at the crowd, her head swaying drunkenly on her shoulders. Someone held up Jilly's arm.

"Nice tits," said a man next to Gunn.

He grinned, started to collect his bets.

Then he remembered Jason Berryman.

It would be damned tough to track the man at night. But he would track him. For now, Jilly needed his attention. He worked his way through the crowd, accepting the payoffs as he went. His pockets were stuffed with bills.

He whipped off his vest, let Jilly slip her arms through the sleeves. It hung there, loose over her pert saucy breasts.

"You won," he said. "Now let's get the hell out of here."

Jilly was beaming with pride. She raised her hands and clasped them over her head in a victory gesture.

The crowd bellowed up a full cheer.

Someone handed Jilly a glass of whiskey. She downed half of it and then her eyes drooped. She collapsed in Gunn's arms. He lifted her up and started toward the batwing doors.

"Goodnight!" he said. "Little champ's gonna leave the gym!"

For years, the Settlement would talk about that night. The poker game and the wildcat fight. And the beautiful breasts of two game women. It was something the townspeople would never forget. It elevated Gunn, Amy and Jilly to legend. The stories of that night, suitably embellished, were to be heard over many a campfire throughout the west.

Amy's supporters saw to it that she got home, after buying her several rounds of losers' drinks. She didn't mind. It helped ease the pain.

Jason was waiting for Amy when they brought

her home in the buckboard.

He stood in the shadows until the two men and a woman had left.

He waited a while longer to make sure that she hadn't been followed. He was puzzled. The three people had carried Amy inside her home. Or almost carried her. They had had to hold her up. And Amy was singing and cursing, alternatively, at the top of her voice.

When it was quiet again, he went up to the porch, knocked on the door.

"Amy! Amy! Let me in! It's Jason."

When the door opened, he could smell the aroma of coffee. Amy was in her gown. Her eyes were puffy, red-rimmed. Blue bruises on her neck and shoulders. Scratches on her chin and jaw. She held a cup of steaming coffee in her hand.

"Come in, Jason." Her tongue was thick, the words slightly slurred.

He drank coffee with her, pleaded his case.

Amy listened to every word. The coffee helped clear her mind, burn out some of the whiskey taste in her mouth. As Jason talked, she wondered how she could have been so fooled by him, so blind to his real character. He was smooth. Slick. He talked a blue streak. Her mind drifted back to the night she had let him make love to her. He had talked that way then. He had a pleasant voice. A lulling tone to it. Now, though, instead of being hypnotized by it, she began to grow sober. She heard

Jason tell her about Jilly Collins. He had jilted her and she'd made up a lot of lies about him. Now she'd hired a gunman, a bad man probably wanted by the law, to extort money from him. He, Jason, was a legitimate businessman, being hounded by a crazy woman. He loved Amy, only Amy, and she must help him kill Gunn so that they could get married and live in peace.

Jason's head was wreathed in smoke. He was on his second cheroot, his first cup of coffee.

"I rest my case," he said. "I made my break because I figured Gunn was going to shoot me under the table. He stacked the deck and tried to hang all that on me about Jilly and her money. I never took a dime from her or any other woman. You've got to believe that, Amy."

"You finished?" Amy asked. Her tone was flat, with just a trace of weariness.

"I guess I am. I shouldn't have to defend myself against a killer like Gunn. Against a card cheat."

"I have some things to say, Jason. And then I want you to get out."

His eyes narrowed. Anger flickered at the corners, but he suppressed it.

"Go ahead, Amy."

"First of all, Jason, you haven't once asked me why I'm so beat up, nor offered me any sympathy. Not that I want any, but it tells me something. I think you were afraid to ask. I'm going to tell you why I look like I've been on a week's drunk. I fought with Jilly Collins tonight. Defending your honor, you sonofabitch. No, wait, let me finish." Jason started to interrupt, but Amy held up a hand to stay him.

"She fought like a tigress. She beat me. And I outweigh her more than a few pennyweight. It dawned on me, after she left, that she fought so well because *she was in the right*. She won for the same reason.

"As for Gunn. He didn't cheat you. He beat you fair and square. It was your deal. He didn't even cut the cards. He had you cold. All the way. Because *he was in the right*.

"You say you've never beaten any woman out of money, but you wanted to borrow fifteen thousand from me, Jason. I was gullible enough to believe you. I saw a real man tonight. The one you say is riffraff. You call him a liar and a card cheat.

"Yet Gunn met you face to face in front of everyone. It didn't dawn on me until I started to sober up and after you had started your explanation of everything. Gunn wasn't afraid of you. He came to that game deliberately. He led you right smack up against your own greed. You were out to clean his whistle, but he was out to show you up for what you were. He won and you welched on your bet. You took that note. You ran like a coward."

She finished her coffee, stood up. She looked

down at Jason. Looked at him with pity.

"Amy, no. You've got it all twisted. I told you . . ."

"Jason, please. Don't make it any worse. Somehow, I knew you'd be here tonight. I knew you'd try to weasel your way back into my affections, try to salvage what you could." She reached down and pulled up her gown. There was a Smith & Wesson pocket .32 in a holster strapped to her leg. She drew the pistol, cocked it. "I'm going to give you this chance, let you ride out of here, instead of turning you in to the sheriff. If you hurry, you might get away before Gunn gets on your trail."

Jason's jaw hardened.

"I've done nothing wrong," he stonewalled. "You've got to . . ."

"Jason, listen. Listen real close. After Gunn and Jilly left, the sheriff came to the saloon. Looking for you. He's got two men locked up. One is named Amos Dunbar. I know him. He works at the Coeur d'Alene. Or did. The other is a gunman named Bruce Gentry."

"Bruce . . . ?"

"They call him Bud. He's wanted in about four states. The point is that both these men are talking about you, Jason. Don't bother to deny any of it. The sheriff believes them. So do I."

"Amy . . . Gunn cleaned me out . . . I—I don't have any money . . . I—I'm begging you . . ."

She thought she was going to be sick.

"No, Jason. Not a cent. Get out. If I see you in my house or outside, I'll shoot you down as I would a rattlesnake or a skunk." She waved the barrel of the Smith & Wesson at him.

"I'll get you for this!" Jason snarled. "I'll get you all for this!"

Amy watched him until he appeared on the road, his black horse glistening in the moonlight. She didn't hate Jason anymore.

She hated herself.

CHAPTER TWENTY

"This is all yours, Jilly. All you're likely to get, though."

Gunn counted out the money he had won from Jason, the money he had won betting on Jilly in the fight with Amy. They had made love, tenderly, gingerly. Jilly hurt all over, but she had only cried out in pain a few times. He still had the chips, figured what part of them was his own money, what part was hers.

"I can't accept that money. You won it from Jason."

"He was playing with your money. I don't need it. You do."

"Gunn?"

He lay naked in his bed. Soo Li was in Jilly's room. Asleep, he hoped.

"Yeah?"

"Couldn't it be our money?"

Her hand floated over his belly, down to his crotch. It was tempting. Jilly had style. Like her grandmother. Bloodlines. She was a thoroughbred. Handsome a woman as he'd ever seen. Yet, she was a townie. That was part of her too. She was pretty good stock. Could ride and shoot, probably would fare well on a ranch or farm. But that wasn't in her blood. She was a St. Louis woman and the city would eventually claim her back.

Besides, he was not ready to settle down yet. There were too many places to go, too many places to see. The West was big and it could swallow a man up or a man could leave his mark wherever he went and give something back to a land that gave so much. He didn't love Jilly. He respected her, but that wasn't the same. It was good enough for friendship, but he had no hankering to trade his saddle horse in for a buggy and brace of mules.

He grabbed her hand, squeezed it.

"It can't be, Jilly."

"I know," she said sadly. "I guess I knew from the beginning."

"I'm sorry."

She slid over to him, kissed him impulsively.

"Don't be. You're all haired over, as my father

used to say, but you're half-tame."

They let the silence close around them, envelop their thoughts.

Gunn knew that the business with Jason wasn't finished. He might have cleaned him out of cash, but the man was still loose. He could still prey on defenseless women. For all he knew, Amy was still under his spell. His thoughts drifted to the woman who, a few hours ago, had fought Jilly over Jason. She, too, was a handsome woman. And she seemed to have style. And intelligence. What quality was it in such men that would cause normal intelligent beautiful women to fall head over heels in love? Was it something inside Jason or something inside Amy and Jilly that caused all the trouble, affected sound reasoning? Couldn't the women see beyond the clothes, the face, the words? Couldn't they judge character any better than that? Possibly not. Jason was smooth and he had a certain style of his own. Men could see through it. But not women. Not lonely women. Not open, giving women. Women like Amy and Jilly.

Jason was probably with Amy right at that moment. He was probably worming his way back into her confidence. If she listened to him, she would believe that Jilly had lied. That he had lied. Somehow, after what had happened, he couldn't believe that Amy would fall for Jason's line of hogwash anymore. If she put all the pieces together, she could see him for what he was.

Jason had called him a tinhorn. But Jason was the tinhorn. And worse, he was a killer. He had hired Bud Gentry to murder or kidnap Jilly and Soo Li. That scheme was on the books, had to be accounted for. Gunn meant to find Jason and bring him to justice. The Sheriff might be looking for him, but it was Gunn's responsibility too. He cared very much for both Soo Li and Jilly. As long as Jason was at large, neither of them were safe.

When first light came, he would leave, take up the trail of Jason Berryman.

It felt good to be aboard Buck again.

The horse was frisky in the dawn light as Gunn put him through his paces, switching gaits to let the animal limber up. The morning was crisp, not yet warm, the sky slightly overcast with thin gray scudding clouds.

Jilly had not heard him get up and he had not told her he was leaving. She would know soon enough. He thought of her with tenderness, but he was restless to get this business over with. If Jason was not at Amy Rawlings' place, then he would pick up the trail at the cabin where Bud Gentry had held him and Soo Li prisoner. His saddlebags were packed with cheese, rye bread and a hunk of salt bacon. His canteen was full, hung from the saddle horn. Bedroll behind the cantle, Winchester in its scabbard. He could stay out a long time, if need be. Somehow, he thought Jason would not give up so easily. He had run, sure, but he was a man who would rankle because he had lost everything on the turn of a card. His vanity alone would nag him to recoup that which he had lost. Including Amy Rawlings, if that was the case, and most certainly her money—and Jilly's.

A morning haze lay over the valley. Smoke from the morning cookfires hung like a pall over the settlement, the Mission. The pasture around Amy's place glistened with sunshot dew. The air smelled fresh with the scent of grass and pine and cedar. He circled the house, came up to the stables in the rear. He did not know Amy's stock, but he would find out. He tied Buck to a hitchpost in the yard, looked for fresh tracks around the stable and tack room. There was a set of tracks that were several hours old. Dew-rimmed, the edges just beginning to fall. Five hours maybe. Could have been Jason. He paid special attention to the tracks. Shod horse, big, heavy. Shoes were new, well-defined tracks where the horse had stood. He followed the tracks a ways, saw the way the horse dragged his rear hoofs. The rider had walked the horse, stopped, then ridden on, heading northwest, toward the hills. Toward the cabin where Bud Gentry had stayed.

There were three horses in the stables. Hungry. No one had come out that morning to give them grain or hay. They had water.

He stopped short in the tackroom.

One of the saddles caught his eyes. He walked over to it, rubbed his hands over the worn oiled leather. He became lost in thought, as memories flooded in on him.

"Hold it right there, mister. I've got a shotgun loaded with double ought buck aimed right at your back. You turn around slow."

He recognized the voice.

Amy Rawlings.

The back of his neck crawled. He raised his arms slowly. Turned around.

"Gunn? What are you doing here?"

"I mean you no harm, Miss Rawlings. I'm bound to seek out Jason Berryman. I'm starting here."

"You're hunting Jason? Why? You got your money."

"Some of it. But that's not the point."

"What is the point?"

"Jason tried to kill two women. He kidnapped one of them. A Chinese girl from Dixon name of Soo Li. He also is thousands short of what he now owes Miss Collins. You don't believe me, still?"

"I believe you. You seem pretty interested in that saddle."

Gunn tossed a look over his shoulder.

"I ought to. It's mine. Or was once."

Amy stepped up to him. Dropped the barrels of the shotgun.

"Your saddle? My driver, Andy McAndrew found it on the road near Hell Gate Pass."

"Right where I dropped it. Is it for sale?"

"Come on in the house, Gunn. We'll discuss it. And some other things, too, if you've the time."

"I'll take the time," he grinned, "if you'll unload that piece in your hands."

Amy cracked the shotgun, pulled out the two shotgun shells. The swelling over her eyes had gone down. She had a mouse on the lid of one of them. She smelled of fresh powder, some kind of musky perfume. Her short blond hair was combed neatly. She wore a man's linsey woolsey shirt, faded Levi's, beaded moccasins. Gunn helped her lay out feed for her horses before they went into the house.

"Breakfast, Gunn?"

"I like to hunt on an empty stomach. Keeps me from getting logy."

"You're used to this, aren't you?"

"Some. You still sweet on Jason?"

Amy poured fresh made coffee into two porcelain cups. The aroma made Gunn slightly dizzy.

She sat down, looked him straight in the eye.

"Not any more. I know what kind of man Jason is. Now. I was blind before. What I don't understand is what your interest is. Are you and Miss Collins . . . ?"

"No. Nothing like that. I was heading this way and our trails crossed. Jason forced a Chinese couple to go against their natures and almost murder Jilly. So I got into it." He told Amy the story of

222

Jilly's near drowning, the kidnapping of Soo Li, his capture by Bud Gentry. She listened with growing horror. Her hand went to her neck, massaged it as a man might if he had narrowly escaped having his throat cut or being hanged.

"I guess you must think I'm a pretty big fool, Mr. Gunn."

"No. Jilly is an intelligent woman. I can't explain men like Jason Berryman. But they're like a canker on the face of the earth. He should have had his lights put out a long time ago. Instead, he just goes on, sweet-talking every woman he meets out of her purse, her savings."

"I'm grateful to you, Gunn. You opened my eyes. You and your friend Jilly."

"No thanks necessary. Now, I'd better get back on Jason's track. Thanks for the coffee, ma'am. I'd like to deal you out of that saddle when I get finished, though. I've rode that a long time over a heap of country."

"The saddle's yours, Gunn. But I hope you won't leave. I'd like to show my gratitude in a more personal way."

Before he knew what was happening, Amy had her arms around his neck, was kissing him desperately on the face and mouth. He struggled for a moment until he realized the depth of her need. Amy was weeping quietly, hungering for him. His heart reached out for her. He knew that hunger, that need. She was a fullblown woman and her ponderous breasts were flattening against his chest, her thighs pressing against his.

"I want you, Gunn," she husked, trying to control her sobbing. "God, how I want you. Jason has left me crushed, broken, lost. Please don't say no. Not now. Later, but not now."

"Jesus, Miss Rawlings!"

"Please!"

He was helpless. When a woman cried like that, he had no words, no backbone. He was just jelly. Her mouth went to his neck, worried his flesh. Her nose burrowed into a spot behind his ear and his gut fluttered with antic moths.

He let himself be led upstairs to her bedroom. Jason would have to wait.

He was surprised at himself. That he could be aroused so soon after leaving Jilly. Let Amy was another woman and this was another time. His loins stirred with desire when he saw her naked body, the lightcolored thatch of hair between her legs, the huge melony breasts, the comely freckles sprinkled over her body. Her face was flushed with passion, her arms beckoning.

In bed, he kissed her breasts, teased the brown thumbsized nipples with his tongue. She squirmed in delight, the tears gone. She grasped his swollen cock and jacked it with a sudden spurt of energy. Fresh blood flowed into the purple veins that wound around his stalk. Her nipples hardened into chinquapins. The dark aureoles flared with bumps. Her freckles changed hues, her flesh appeared to be broken out in a flaming rash.

"I get this way when I'm excited," she breathed. "It's all right."

"I want this inside me, Gunn. I want you to fuck me. Fuck me hard."

Her words roused his passions, smothered the last of his hesitancy.

He mounted her, slipped into her sheath. She sighed, bucked with a sudden orgasm as soon as he passed the labial portal. He slid across the button and she bucked again, clamping her arms around his back. Her legs swung up in the air and he sank deep.

There seemed no end to her. Her wide hips caved in as he pounded into her. She seemed perfectly formed to enclose his own form within hers.

He rattled her senses with every stroke. She rocked him in her arms as if he was a child. Her large breasts flowed over her chest like massive mounds of pudding. Her fingers dug into his back, and her legs kept him snug inside her.

She climaxed several times. Still, Gunn held back. This surprised her.

She noted the contrast between Jason's lovemaking and Gunn's. She might not have noticed the difference had Gunn not bedded her, but it was startling. Jason had thought only of himself. He was hurried, crude. There was a cold part to him, a reserve that she now realized was not just shyness or inexperience, but a part of his personality. Gunn gave her all he had and withheld his own pleasure to satisfy her.

She struggled, then, to make him release his seed. It became both a challenge and a game. She wriggled her hips, pumped upward with vigorous bursts of her pelvis. She skewered him into her and still he came on, driving, pounding, searing parts of her that jolted her senses with electric charges. She gasped and sighed, screamed in ecstasy.

"My god, what a man!" she breathed at one point.

"I hope you're happy, Amy."

"Yes, yes, oh my god, I've never been fucked like this before!"

He let her frolic until she was soaked with her sweat and his. He could have lasted all day, but he had things to do. There were limits to everything. When she was ready for him, he stroked her quick and deep until his seed exploded and burst inside her. She clutched him as a desperate woman will clutch a man and held him through the spasmic convulsions that followed ejaculation.

Once again, tears flooded her eyes.

Tears of gratitude.

He left her, after a time.

He made no promises. She waved goodbye from the porch as he rode toward the hills above the Mission.

He waved back.

He was not worried about Amy. She would be all right. She would find the man she wanted.

He would have to be a pretty good man, too.

He hoped she would find him soon. It was a shame to let a woman like Amy go lonesome.

CHAPTER TWENTY-ONE

Jason looked out at the predawn night with raw eyes.

Sleep had been a fitful tossing and turning. Nightmare-ridden. He slept, fully clothed, in the back bedroom of the cabin, his fingers wrapped around the butt of his pistol. Every sound had startled him awake. The wind, the creak of boards, the far off bark of a dog, all had made his night into something unreal, grotesque.

But Gunn hadn't come.

Not yet.

He dared not light a fire. He nibbled on stale rice, dried beef. He lathered his beard with cold water and lye soap, winced as he scraped the stubble down to the flesh with a straight razor. Quickly, he packed his saddlebags with dried fruit, jerky, biscuits you couldn't drive a nail through, extra flour, coffee. He stuffed the coffee pot with towels, packed it, too. It wouldn't rattle.

The pale cream light began to spread across the morning sky. Jason's nerves jangled like a shopful of alarm clocks all going off at the same time.

He had to get moving.

He felt rested, refreshed after the food, the shave and a face wash.

The black was fed, watered. He saddled him, tied on his bedroll, snugged the saddlebags down. He had cartridges in his pockets for pistol and rifle. He stuffed heavy cord, twine and rags in the saddlebags, as well. He would need these things later.

Everything was set.

It would take him a long time to do what he had to do, but it was the only way.

Gunn would track him, he knew that. But he'd follow a false trail.

He would have to summon up every bit of trail lore he remembered and some he had forgotten, he knew. In order to shake Gunn off and do what he had to do. And time was running out on him. Fast!

When he was set, Jason mounted up. Rode away from the cabin. He left plenty of sign that he had been there. He made no attempt to hide his tracks now. He let the black, whom he called Satan, frisk all he wanted. Let his hooves jar loose stones on the trail, scrape the dust, crush the grass and brush. An easy trail to follow. It would be, for a time. Then, he hoped, the trail would become confusing to a tracker. Would mislead Gunn long enough for him to finish his business in the settlement. He rode fast, then, needing the distance to accomplish the first part of his plan.

Jason headed toward Coeur d'Alene lake and Spokane, following the old Mullan Road along the N.P. tracks. He rode fast once he cleared sight of the Mission. Satan was sound. He could do what Jason demanded.

As the sun rose in the hills, Jason beat a clear path west. He rode for an hour, two. Then, he took to the brush, south to Hangman Creek. He rode into the creek, still heading south and then back out again as the creek surged easterly. In and out, making sure the tracks always returned to the earth, then back into the creek. He crossed over, left the creek, headed toward Walla Walla. There he stopped. He cut brush and looped heavy cord through the cut end, wrapped them tightly together. He remounted and began his drag. Gunn, he knew, could follow the drag as easily as he could the hoof marks in thick dust.

Some distance further on, Jason dismounted again. He pulled the roll of twine and rags from his saddlebags, knelt down by his horse's hind hooves. He wrapped each hoof with thick layers of rags and tied them around the hocks with the heavy twine. He put rags on all four hooves.

Mounted again, Jason rode with the drag a while longer, then dropped the brush and rode Satan on a little further, checking the marks the hooves made. Not much. Satisfied, he sidestepped the black horse north, made a wide loop, following stony ground as much as he could until he reached Hangman Creek again. Traveling north, he left no visible tracks on the east side of the creek.

Once he reached the east end of the lake, he made a loop around it, to the north.

If everything worked out, he would reach the settlement again under cover of darkness.

Then, he would do those things he had planned. He would start to quell the rage that blazed in him like a runaway timber fire.

And Gunn would be far away, lost in a maze of false trails!

* * *

The tracks were too easy to follow.

Gunn wasn't worried. Not at first. Jason was citybred, probably wanted to leave the Mission as fast as possible.

Then why had he spent the night in the cabin? That bothered him.

Jason had been there all right. He left his smell on the bedclothes. Fresh spilled water from the pitcher, in the bowl. Wet razor.

Horse tracks fresh. No more than an hour or so old.

He ought to be able to catch up before dark. Maybe sooner if Jason kept the same pace or tried to slow him down by messing up the trail.

Gunn felt guilty about being with Amy. Had he not spent so long there he might have surprised Jason at the cabin. Or would he have? The more he tracked, the more it seemed that Jason had left before dawn or about then. A couple of hours ahead instead of just one. Still, he had lost time and he regretted it now.

Jason was a greenhorn, it appeared. He was taking a direct line to Spokane, following the road, as if he didn't give a damn.

Then, the tracks went off the trail.

Gunn felt a twinge of suspicion.

Why?

The high clouds began to blow off, drift easterly. The sun burned through the mountain haze and Gunn had clear vision for miles. It bothered him that Jason had left the road, but there could be a reason. Either he believed he would be followed or he knew he would be followed.

Gunn stood up in the saddle, scanned the countryside. It was rocky, brushstrewn. Yet Jason still left a clear trail, holding to the open spaces. There was something clawing at his mind for recognition, but he couldn't get a handle on it. Something important. Something just beyond his reach, his grasp.

From that point on, Gunn grew increasingly wary. His eyes darted everywhere. Every rock pile, every clump of brush, every tree was a potential hiding place. A place for ambush. The heat made him sweat. The trail led down to Hangman Creek. He saw where Jason rode into the stream. Trying to shake him off? The tracks appeared every so often, back on dry land. Then back into the creek.

He lost them for a time, had to backtrack on the opposite side.

The time ticked away. The hours stretched.

Gunn cursed.

Something was wrong, but he couldn't figure out what it was.

He picked up the trail, finally, past noon.

Jason was heading west again.

After following the easterly course of the creek?

Either the man was crazy or he had something up his damned sleeve!

Gunn's stomach was hollow. He could almost feel something inside gnawing at him. In his gut, in his brain.

He found the place where Jason had stopped and cut brush.

What the hell!

Gunn stopped, too. He slabbed a chunk of cheese on a piece of rye bread, nibbled it thoughtfully.

He rode on, slowly, following the brushed trail. A tic started up in his jaw. His mouth tasted as dry as a hundred year old bone. His stomach continued to feed some gnawing shadow of animal, some invisible creature that kept trying to crawl into his brain and gain his attention. The terrain roughened, but always, Jason kept to the open places. The brush was a hindrance. It slowed the man down unnecessarily. Was Jason really such a fool? Was he really that much of a tenderfoot?

And then, Gunn came upon the next place Jason had stopped.

This puzzled him even more.

He dismounted, studied the ground.

Jason's boot marks were plain to see. He had done something. Checked his horse's hooves? There was some evidence of that.

Gunn remounted, followed the brush tracks.

He paused when he saw the pile of brush lying in the trail.

Jason had abandoned that ruse. Why? Too heavy? Too much trouble? Too fruitless? Had he finally gotten some sense in his head? Possibly.

The tracks petered out. It took Gunn the better part of an hour to figure them out. Now he knew why Jason had stopped back there. He had put cloth on his horse's hooves. An old Indian trick. Good under certain circumstances. Still, in this country, the mark of a tenderfoot.

Jason was up to something. He *was* thinking—even if his thinking was muddled. He was thinking very hard. Going to a hell of a lot of trouble to mislead him, shake him off.

He had wasted hours on this trail. The sun was starting to fall away in the sky.

Had Jason gone on, then, to Walla Walla? Or doubled back north to Spokane? Neither course made much sense.

Gunn decided to follow the new tracks further. He would know for sure soon. But that elusive something clamoring for attention in his brain was beginning to draw nearer. It was growing a handle.

It was only a question of time.

The tracks led back to the stream. Hangman Creek.

Up or down?

Down would make no sense.

Gunn headed north.

He came upon the place where Jason's horse had sogged back up out of the stream. He found bits of cloth clinging to brush.

Sonofabitch!

Lake Coeur d'Alene shimmered in the waning afternoon sunlight. The tracks followed its western edge. There was no need to follow them.

He knew now what his gut had been trying to tell him. He grabbed the handle, saw it all clear.

Jason Berryman was going back to Mission Cataldo.

Gunn looked up at the sky. He knew the general size of the lake, knew how long it would take to ride around the lake if a man hurried. Or if he wanted to get into the settlement at a certain time—after dark!

"Come on boy," Gunn said to Buck. "You ought to be ready for a ride. You've been loafing your ass off all day."

Spurs dug into Buck's flanks as Gunn whipped the reins, turning the horse back toward the settlement. Buck responded, digging in his hooves as he leaped ahead.

Gunn's jaw stopped twitching. The gnawing had gone away.

Now his gut crawled with fear.

Jason had foxed him. Jilly was in danger. And maybe, Amy and Soo Li, as well.

The wind whipped at him as he rode.

The sun crawled down the sky, heading for the sea.

"I can't wait a minute longer, Soo Li," Jilly said. "It's getting late. I have to find out if anyone has seen or heard from Gunn."

"He did not leave note or anything?"

"No. He was just gone. I've looked all over for him. Someone said he had gone to Amy Rawlings place early this morning. She'll be back at Stillman's after dark. Maybe she can tell us something."

"You want me to go with you?"

"Yes, you might as well. Do you want a pistol? I'm going to carry the Starr with me. Something's wrong, terribly wrong."

"I will go. No pistol. They scare me."

Jilly laughed. She had chewed her fingernails all day long. She hoped that Amy would have some news. Besides, she wanted to apologize to the lady. It wasn't her fault that Jason had hoodwinked her, too.

As the two women were leaving the hotel, the stage from Dixon roared up in a cloud of dust. The driver, Andy McAndrew, shouted to the team, drew up the brake, wrapped the reins around it.

"Jilly!"

Jilly stopped.

Stared at the stage. Out of it stepped Doctor Percival Merriwether. He stood there, reached inside the coach. Abigail Evanston stepped down, a wide grin on her face.

"My god, Soo Li, I almost forgot about my grandmother!"

Before Soo Li could say anything, Jilly had raced down the steps, her arms outstretched. Abigail screamed with delight. Jilly whooped as she took the old lady in her arms.

Bud sat up on the jail cot.

A low whistle sounded outside.

He looked over at Amos Dunbar. His shoulder was bandaged. His hand, too. The doctor had given him something for pain. Nothing for the hate he carried inside.

"Did you hear something, Dunbar?"

"Just kids. Playin' out back."

The whistle sounded again.

"Bud?" a voice whispered.

"It's Jason!" Bud said to Dunbar, keeping his voice low. "He's come to break us out."

"How?"

"I dunno. Quick, help me up to the window."

Dunbar helped Bud Gentry climb on the cot.

"Jason? That you out there?"

"Bud, it's me. Dunbar in there with you?"

"Yeah."

A face appeared outside the jail window. Bud leaned forward. Jason rode up close on his black horse. There was an explosion and half of Gentry's face was blown away. A fine spray blew out of the back of his head, splattering Dunbar with a hot red mist.

Gentry was blown backwards. The pistol came through the bars, exploded again. Dunbar started to scream. Nothing came out. A blueblack hole appeared in his throat. He gurgled, twitched, then fell. His blood sobbed out on the jail floor as shouts were heard from the office.

Gentry and Dunbar heard nothing.

CHAPTER TWENTY-TWO

The street was boiling with people as Gunn rode into the settlement.

Was he too late?

From the looks of the town, all hell had broken loose. The main concentration seemed to be in front of the sheriff's office. That's where the jail was. Gunn rode up there, hitched Buck to the rail in front of the post office, next door.

He waded through the crowd.

"What's going on here?" he asked.

"Coupla fellers got shot in the jail there," said a man who recognized Gunn.

"Who did it?"

"They don't know."

"You see Miss Collins anywhere?"

"Why, yes. She and a couple of other ladies, and a man, too, come to think of it, was headed down the street. Jest after it happened." The man pointed toward Stillman's.

"Thanks, pardner."

Jason went into the jail. The sheriff and his deputy looked harried.

"What happened?" Gunn asked.

The sheriff told him.

Gunn went back, looked at the two men.

"Figured someone shot 'em through the jail window. Killed 'em stone dead."

"Jason Berryman," Gunn said.

"Huh? You witness it?"

"No, but the sonofabitch doubled back here. He doesn't want any witnesses."

"Well, hell, where is he?" Butterfield asked.

"I don't know, sheriff. But I aim to find out."

Before the sheriff could stop him, Gunn was gone.

"It's a mess," said Butterfield. "A damned mess. Deputy, help me get this crowd the hell home."

Stillman's was becoming jammed.

People streamed in off the streets, talking of the double murder in the jail. None of them had put Jason's name to the killings because they did not know of the connection.

Jilly did, however.

"When I first heard the shots, my heart jumped up in my throat," she told her grandmother, the others. "I—I guess I'm jumpy. I thought Gunn had been killed."

"Now, child," said Abigail. "You mustn't worry so. Gunn can handle himself."

"But where is he? Maybe Jason killed him so that he doesn't have to worry any more. Maybe he's come back to kill all of us. One by one."

"I'm sure that's a little far-fetched," said Doctor Merriwether. "Surely the man is not that insane."

Jilly gave Merriwether a look of utter pity. The four of them sat at a table near one of the four front windows. Amy Rawlings still had not showed. She and her grandmother had kissed each other silly. Then she had introduced Soo Li to Abigail and the doctor. They had brought news of Soo Li's parents. They were going to drop the attempted murder charges, but were to be deported back to China. They would be taken by stage to San Francisco next week. If Soo Li wanted to go with them, she was welcome to return. Her passage would be paid by the U.S. Government, as well. Soo Li had made no comment. Jilly's grandmother had arranged for a room, adjoining the doctor's and they had agreed to go to Stillman's for drinks, then all have dinner together. The shooting had occurred as they were walking towards Stillman's.

"You don't know how vicious Jason is," Jilly said. "But just remember that he hired that man who shot my grandmother. He also kidnapped Soo Li here and forced her parents to almost become murderers. And, most likely, Jason shot those two men in the jail. He hired them to kill both me and Soo Li.

"Incredible," said the doctor.

"Aw come on, Percy, drink up," said Abigail. "I feel like tying one on tonight. At least, Jilly, you're safe. Mr. Gunn will turn up, I'm sure."

Jilly was morose and inconsolable. She sipped her whiskey disconsolately. Soo Li did not drink, but sat there, prim and quiet, thinking about her parents.

Amy Rawlings came in the saloon through the back hallway. She looked around anxiously before Jilly spotted her. Jilly waved, stood up.

"Over here!" she called, above the din.

Amy's face was chalk white. Her skin looked even paler than usual. She wore a light cotton dress of dark gray. The moment she walked up, Jilly knew something was wrong.

"Miss Rawlings . . . have you . . ."

Amy held up her hand.

"Please, Miss Collins. Jilly. I must talk to you. Alone. It's—it's very important."

Jilly excused herself and left the table.

"What's the matter?" she asked when they were standing alone by the hallways.

Amy's eyes were wide. She was trembling. She appeared on the verge of tears.

"Jilly. How much money do you have on your person?"

Jilly looked down at her purse, a look of confusion on her face.

"Why—why a little over twenty thousand, I suppose. I should put it in the hotel safe, but . . ."

"Never mind. Can I have it? Please?"

"What's wrong? Are you in trouble?"

Amy's eyes darted to the back of the saloon, down the hall.

She lowered her voice.

"Jason's got my driver, Andy. He's going to cut his throat unless I bring him forty thousand dollars. I—I've only got about fifteen thousand on hand. God, I don't know what to do!"

"Where's Gunn? Have you seen him?"

"Not since this morning. Please, Jilly. He gave me ten minutes. He'll kill Andy. He's wild-eyed and desperate."

"Where's Jason?"

"Out back. If I'm not there . . ."

She didn't finish. Jason stalked down the hall, a gun at Andy McAndrews' back. Jilly saw him before Amy did. Quickly, she shoved Amy out of the way. Amy screamed, wondering what was happening. Jilly opened her purse, groped for the big caliber Starr.

Jason shot from underneath Andy's arm. The bullet creased the air, buzzing over Jilly's head. It hit the window where Abigail, Soo Li and the doctor sat. People in the saloon dove for the floor. There were cries and screams.

At that moment, Gunn walked in the front door.

Jason saw him, fired a shot in his direction.

Gunn threw himself headlong, drawing his pistol.

Amy struggled to her feet.

"Get down!" warned Jilly, drawing her pistol.

Jason fired a shot into Andy's back, shoved him straight at Jilly.

244

Granny Evanston saw what was happening. She drew her own hideout pistol from her purse. She aimed at Jason, fired.

Jason was already moving. He grabbed Jilly, knocked the Starr from her hand. The pistol skidded through the sawdust, landed in front of Amy. Amy stared at it for a long moment, then grasped it in shaking hands.

Jason grabbed Jilly around the neck, snatched her purse from her hand.

Gunn rose to his feet. People in the center of the room crawled toward the edges. Others dashed through the batwing doors during the lull.

Gunn was unable to fire, afraid of hitting Jilly.

Jilly's eyes went wide with terror. Jason's arms ground into her neck, shutting off her wind.

"Leave her be, Jason!"

Jason whirled, saw Amy rising to her feet, the black barrel of the Starr pointing at him. He fired pointblank, whirled again, his back to the hallway. He started backing away. Amy took a step toward him, dropped the pistol. She pitched forward, a hole in her breast. Jilly pushed at Jason, then bit his arm. He howled in pain, released her.

Jason started after her.

Gunn still couldn't get a clear shot. But Granny moved in, waiting for her chance.

Jilly stuck her leg out. Jason tripped over it, sprawled in the center of the room. Jilly scrambled for her pistol. She picked it up as Jason got to his feet, spun in her direction.

Granny had moved in close.

She shot Jason in the hip.

He twisted slightly, fired a shot in the air.

Jilly circled Jason.

Gunn tried again for a shot, but Granny was in the way on one side, Jilly on the other.

He cursed his luck.

"You sonofabitch!" yelled Jilly. "Drop your gun!"

Jason, his eyes glazed with pain, flashed her a murderous look, then brought his pistol up to fire at her.

She and her grandmother fired at Jason simultaneously. They fired again and again, hammering back coolly, taking deliberate aim. Neither of them tried for a killing shot. It was like a ballet that had been planned in advance. It was beautiful and horrible. Gunn saw it in a terrible slow motion that he was powerless to stop.

Jason danced like a man having the fits as bullets ripped into his legs and arms. He didn't fall. He twisted one way. A shot drew him up and spun him another way. The shots were evenly spaced. He fired once more, hitting Abigail in her good arm. She winced, and shot him again.

Jilly fired her last shot into Jason's groin.

Granny's pistol was empty, smoking in her hand.

Gunn ran up, then, but Jason's legs collapsed under him. He fell backwards in an awkward sprawl, his pistol still in his hand. His fingers twitched around the butt. He stared up at Jilly with watery eyes, eyes that were filming over. Blood gushed from a half dozen wounds. Gunn saw that he wasn't going to make it. He reached down, jerked the pistol from his grasp. Then, he looked at Jilly and her grandmother, saw that they were all right. He holstered his own pistol, now useless, and went to Amy.

He held the dying woman in his arms.

Blood bubbled up in her mouth. Twin trickles oozed from the corners. He wiped the blood away. Kissed her tenderly on the lips.

"I—it's bad, isn't it?" she said.

"Don't try to talk, Amy. We've a doctor here."

Percival Merriwether came up, loomed over them. He looked at Gunn, shook his head. Amy saw the gesture, nodded.

"I would have liked to have known you first, Gunn," she rasped.

"Me too. Go with God, huh?"

"Did—did they get Jason?"

Gunn nodded.

"He's dying."

"With my luck, I'll go with Jason," she said, attempting a smile. Gunn's heart wrenched in his chest.

"Do you want a priest, Amy?"

"No. It's too late for that. Kiss me again, will you?"

Jilly came up, heard her words. She looked as Gunn bent his head. He put his lips on Amy's. Her body gave a shudder. He squeezed her one last time, lay her head down gently. He stripped off his vest, wadded it up and tucked it under her head for a pillow.

"Goodbye, Amy." There was a catch in his throat. He stood up, watery-eyed.

"Is that sonofabitch dead yet?" he croaked.

"He's dead," said Jilly, touching Gunn's arm.

"My only regret is," he said, "that I didn't kill him."

Jilly picked up her purse. She told Gunn that Jason probably had some of Amy's money on him. By then, the sheriff and his deputy had arrived and taken charge. They were busy taking statements. Doctor Merriwether attended Abigail. Her wound was not serious, but would require dressing. He led her out of the saloon, back to the hotel. People were quiet, whispering in the awesome presence of death. Andy McAndrews was badly wounded, but would probably live. The settlement doctor came and they carried the stage driver out on a cot. The saloon reeked of blood and fear.

"I need a drink," Gunn said. "How about you?"

"I could use something," Jilly said.

Soo Li, who had been under the table the whole time, came up.

"I'm going back to the hotel," she said. "I need time to think, to pack. I'm glad it's over."

"I am too, Soo Li," said Jilly. "Will you go to China with your parents?"

"I don't think so. But I want to see them before they go."

"Maybe we'll ride back to Dixon with you," said Jilly. "I'll see you in a while."

Jilly and Gunn went to the bar. The bartender was solemn, but he said the drinks were on the house.

"Amy would have wanted it that way," he said. "I don't know what we'll do without her." He was weeping openly as were all of the other men lined up for glasses of fortitude.

"Well, Gunn, it's over," said Jilly. "I wish you would come back to St. Louis with me."

"You know I couldn't do that. I'm on my way to Oregon in the morning."

"So soon?"

"So soon." He looked at Jilly, wondering, more than ever, what made her tick. He couldn't wipe the image of Jason's death out of his mind. How she methodically blew holes in him. He shuddered with the memory of it.

Jilly reached into her purse, pulled out the Starr, some bullets. Calmly, she began reloading it.

"I could make you come with me," she said, winking at him.

Gunn gulped.

"You could at that, Jilly," he said. "But we'd both ruin some good memories if you did."

"Will you kiss me, then? Promise to look me up if you're ever in St. Louis?"

"I will." He kissed her. A long time. No one said anything.

Suddenly he was very tired. It had been a hard trail that day. Jason had outwitted him right up to the last. He and Gunn had never had to face each other. Jilly and her grandmother had taken care of that. It was spooky. He knew one thing.

He would never forget Jilly Collins.

Or her grandmother.

EPILOGUE

The stage was loaded, ready to drive to Dixon.

Gunn sat atop Buck, his old saddle under him.

Jilly, Abigail and Merriwether stood by the Concord, waiting to board.

"Where's Soo Li?" Gunn asked. "I wanted to say goodbye to her."

"She told me she hates goodbyes," said Jilly. "She wants to wait until you leave."

"I'm going then. Goodbye, Abigail. Doc. You take care of her. Might see you both in San Francisco one day. Jilly."

"Gunn."

He choked up, clicked his teeth, tapped Buck's flanks with his spurs.

He remembered what Jilly had said, in jest, last night. That she could force him to go with her. At gunpoint. It was an odd thing to joke about.

As he rode down the street, headed west, he kept thinking about his back. About Jilly standing there, that Starr loaded and in her purse. What a nice target his back would make.

A woman scorned.

At the corner of the block, he turned, looked back at her. Abigail and the doctor were boarding the coach.

Jilly was waving at him.

Sadly. There was no pistol in her hand.

He let out a soft sigh.

He waved back, then spurred Buck again. It felt good to have him rocking beneath him again.

He didn't look back. The stage was headed in the opposite direction.

He was free.

At the far edge of Couer d'Alene Lake, Gunn stopped. For the past hour he'd had the odd feeling that someone was following him. Yet, whenever he turned around in the saddle, he saw no one. It was too early for the stage.

Now, he waited, munching on a piece of cheese and half a slice of rye bread.

Yes, someone was back there. Coming on slow,

but steady.

The dot loomed larger and larger.

Finally, he made out the face. He didn't believe it. But it was so. He stretched out, then. There was no hurry.

Soo Li rode up on Jason's black horse, smiled down at him.

Gunn smiled back.

HORROR BESTSELLERS
by J.N. Williamson
FOR THOSE COLD, LONELY NIGHTS!

DEATH-COACH (805, $2.95)
A young woman and her children become the innocent victims of horrifying evil when they move into a small quiet town inhabited by the bloodthirsty Queen of Vampires, Lamia Zacharius.

DEATH-ANGEL (909, $2.95)
Disguised as a beautiful woman, Lamia Zacharius, the three-thousand-year-old vampire, creates the most monstrous child the world has ever known.

DEATH-SCHOOL (981, $2.95)
Thessaly's lovely new school teacher is the deadly vampire Lamia Zacharius—and the children are headed for a horrifying course of evil from which there is no return!

DEATH-DOCTOR (1108, $2.95)
As the lovely "doctor" Lamia Zacharius, Queen of the Vampires, cradles a scarlet-eyed infant in her arms she croons with hideous delight. For this newborn is the essence of all that is evil: a deadly, horrifying demon who hungers for fresh human blood . . .

Available wherever paperbacks are sold, or order direct from the Publisher. Send cover price plus 50¢ per copy for mailing and handling to Zebra Books, 475 Park Avenue South, New York, N.Y. 10016. DO NOT SEND CASH.